MURDER GOES ON TOUR

ROBERT BATY

Copyright (C) 2021 Robert Baty

Layout design and Copyright (C) 2021 by Next Chapter

Published 2021 by Gumshoe – A Next Chapter Imprint

Edited by Sarah Newton-John

Cover art by CoverMint

For Gail

We had a wonderful time on the tour. Who knew that murder could be so much fun?

PETE AND SALLY WILKERSON, DALLAS, TX

ONE

VIVIAN TURNED AWAY FROM THE WOMAN BESIDE HER AND SLIPPED OUT of bed. It was 6am in the city of San Francisco, and she had just spent the night with the famous Joanna Rorke. A whirlwind of drinks, desire and two women naked in each other's arms in a penthouse suite on the top floor of the Hyatt Regency.

Well, that was different, Vivian thought, the taste of Joanna still on her tongue. *So different from being with a man.* She glanced at Joanna, who was still asleep. The comforter had fallen away from her breasts, which glowed in the morning light filtering through the blinds. It occurred to Vivian that it might be fun to do it all again sometime. She fumbled in the dark for her clothes and cosmetics, which were in a pile on the floor along with Joanna's things, then went into the bathroom to get dressed. She was an inked brunette in her late 20s, with an oval face, smoky green eyes and a lizard tattoo that snaked down her thigh.

Vivian glanced at herself naked in the mirror, and a sinful smile spread across her face. She'd had her share of hookups with men she hardly knew, but this was the first time she'd ever done it with a woman. And not just any woman, but a woman who was 20 years older and a bestselling author.

Vivian thought authors rocked. She followed her favorites like groupies trailed pop stars. It wasn't enough for her to read an author's books – those were just words on a page. She wanted the thrill that came from seeing them live and hearing their voices. She lived for the moment when they locked eyes as the author signed an autograph that began "To Vivian…," as if the book had been written just for her.

But she'd never wound up in bed with an author, even though she'd fantasized about it if the author happened to be a hunk. She had also wondered from time to time what it would be like to touch a woman's body, to feel a woman touching her. And then, when it finally happened, Vivian was surprised to discover that she could just as easily lose herself with a woman as with a man. She finished dressing and turned off the light, then walked barefoot to the door with her shoes in her hand.

"Leaving so soon, Vivian?"

Vivian looked at Joanna. She had turned back the comforter, revealing her naked body. She was in her late 40s or early 50s, Vivian guessed, with full breasts, dark eyes and glossy black hair that tumbled to her shoulders and was streaked with gray. She was smiling seductively at Vivian, reminding her of a nude she'd seen once painted by some Spanish artist whose name she couldn't remember. Vivian felt something stir, but knew she had to go.

"I didn't want to wake you," Vivian said. "I have to go to work."

"That's no fun," Joanna said. "Wouldn't you rather stay and play with me?"

Vivian smiled. "Yeah, totally. It was hot."

"Your first time?"

Vivian blushed. "Yeah, it was. Why, did it show?"

"Not at all. I never would've known. You sure you have to go?"

"Yeah, I am."

"A kiss goodbye, then?"

Vivian walked over to where Joanna lay. She sat up and pulled Vivian into her arms and gave her a deep, lingering kiss. Vivian let her hand wander across Joanna's breasts and then down between her thighs. She was wet and suddenly Vivian wanted to taste her again. But there was no time – not if she wanted to keep her job.

"You like that?" Joanna asked.

"Yeah, I do."

"So stay."

"I wish I could."

"I'm going to be in town for a few more days…"

"Yeah, I know. You're reading at another stop on the murder tour."

"Perhaps we can get together again before I leave?"

"Yeah, sure," Vivian said. "That would be excellent. You want my number?"

Joanna smiled. "Of course I do."

Vivian jotted down her number on the notepad on the nightstand.

"Until next time then," Joanna said smiling, pulling the comforter up around her.

Vivian smiled. "Can't wait."

Vivian was still buzzing from the heat of the night as she waited for the cable car that would take her up California Street to her apartment atop Nob Hill. A cellphone text alert beeped from inside her purse. The sound puzzled her, as she had her cellphone in her hand. Vivian reached into her purse and was surprised to discover another cellphone buried underneath her cosmetics. She pulled it out and, in the moment before the screen went dark, she read a text from a woman named Laura Neville: "See you soon, my famous friend. Breakfast is on me."

Suddenly, Vivian realized that in her rush to get dressed she had inadvertently taken Joanna's cellphone. She flushed with embarrassment. What a dumb move. She decided to return it immediately with her apologies. She wondered if Joanna would be amused – perhaps even think that Vivian had done it on purpose, just so she could see her again. The thought brought a smile to her face as she walked across the street to the Hyatt Regency and went up to Joanna's room. She knocked on the door and, as she did so, the door swung open.

"Joanna…?" Vivian said, stepping into the room.

Then she saw her.

3

Joanna was still in bed, but half her face was gone and she was swimming in a sea of blood. Blood spatter smeared the walls and windows. The TV was on, tuned to a morning talk show, but the faces on the screen were speckled with blood.

Vivian froze in horror, unable to look away. She wanted to run but could not move. Her stomach turned and she vomited on the carpet.

Then she heard a knock on the door.

"Señora…" a woman said.

Vivian turned and saw a Latina maid in the doorway. Just as the maid saw the blood. Saw Joanna. And screamed.

TWO

"YOU WANT A GLASS OF WATER?"

Vivian shook her head. She felt as if she couldn't stop shaking. Her mouth tasted like vomit. *This isn't happening,* she told herself. It can't be. Images of Joanna kept flashing before her eyes as she sat at a table in a windowless police interrogation room. The two homicide detectives who had detained Vivian at the scene of the crime were in the room with her. Detective Harry Chen, a stocky Asian in a mud-colored suit, and Detective Latoya Bassett, a thin black woman with a tight afro and glasses. Chen sat across from her while Bassett stood by the door.

"Okay, let's cut to the chase," Chen said. "How did you know Joanna Rorke?"

Vivian flinched as Joanna's name slammed into her.

"I didn't really know her, I just went to her reading." Her voice seemed hollow, disconnected, as if someone else was speaking.

"Don't jerk us around, little girl," Bassett said. "You did a lot more than that. We have a maid who placed you at the scene and witnesses who saw you together in the hotel bar after the reading. We figure when the prints and DNA from her room come back from the lab they're gonna have your name all over 'em."

"Do you own a gun?" Chen asked.

Vivian shook her head.

"Okay," Chen said, "let's take it from the top. You spent the night with her, right?"

Vivian nodded, mortified that it was public knowledge. She wanted nothing more than to disappear and never be seen again.

"Did you have sexual relations with the deceased?" Bassett said.

Vivian looked up at her. She felt her stomach turn. Bassett made it sound as if she'd had sex with a corpse. She lowered her eyes and said, "Yes."

"Had you ever had sex with her before?" Chen said.

Vivian shook her head.

"Had you ever met her before?"

"No."

"So what was it, some kind of casual encounter?" Bassett said.

"I told you before. I went to her reading," Vivian said.

"Lots of people went to her reading," Chen said. "How come she ended up in bed with you?"

"I don't know, it just happened," Vivian said, feeling the heat rush into her face.

"Did you like it?" Bassett said.

"Excuse me?" Vivian said. "What's that got to do with it?"

"You tell me," Bassett said. "But here's the thing, Ms. Voss. We ask the questions and you answer them."

Vivian lowered her eyes. "Okay, I liked it."

Chen and Bassett exchanged sideways smirks.

"You got a boyfriend?" Chen said.

Vivian shook her head. "We broke up a couple of weeks ago."

"Why? You decide you like girls better?" Bassett said.

"He was cheating on me."

"Did anyone else join you?" Bassett said.

Vivian looked at her. "What do you mean?"

"I mean a threesome. You and Joanna and somebody else."

Vivian shook her head. "No, nobody else."

"You see anybody when you were leaving?"

Vivian shook her head.

"So you left, realized you took her phone by mistake and went back to return it. Is that right?" Chen said.

Vivian nodded.

"So you just missed him," Bassett said. "Or her."

Vivian looked up at her.

"The killer."

Vivian shuddered.

"Got any idea why somebody wanted her dead?" Chen said.

"How would I know? I didn't even know her." She shook her head. "I just can't believe she's dead..."

"You knew her well enough to jump into bed with her," Bassett said.

Vivian whipped around to Bassett. "How well do you know everybody you have sex with, detective?"

Bassett's face tightened. She glared at Vivian. "Excuse me?"

"Okay, that's enough," Chen said. "Rorke mention anybody who might have had a grudge against her? Any enemies, somebody she was worried about?"

Vivian shook her head. "We had sex, that was it. But there was this woman at the reading... she asked this weird question...it seemed to bother Joanna."

Bassett and Chen exchanged glances.

"What woman?" Bassett said.

"I don't know, some woman."

"What kind of weird question?"

"She asked Joanna if she'd ever read a certain book. She mentioned the title, I think it was called *Tourist Trap,* something like that. Joanna told her she'd never read it, and the woman said, no, you wouldn't have, it was never published. I asked her about it when we were having a drink and she just brushed it off like it was nothing."

Bassett and Chen exchanged glances.

"Did you see this woman again?"

Vivian nodded. "She was in the bar when we were there. She

ordered a drink, then came over to the table and threw it in Joanna's face."

"Why?"

"I don't know."

"What'd she look like?"

"She was blonde, a little overweight, late 30s. I remember she had a southern accent."

"They knew each other?"

"Joanna said she was just some jealous writer, but it was like they knew each other. I mean you don't throw a drink in somebody's face for no reason, right?"

Vivian wondered if the woman's obvious anger at Joanna had gone from throwing a drink in her face to putting a bullet in her head.

"She mention her name?"

Vivian shook her head.

"Then what happened?"

"The bartender threw her out."

"What's Rorke's book about?" Bassett said.

"It's called *The Murder Tour*," Vivian said. "It's about a serial killer who's murdering tourists who go on murder tours. Joanna told me she was going to promote the book by reading at some of the stops on a tour."

"Murder tours," Chen said in disgust. "It's not enough that people suffer and die, somebody's gotta make a buck off it."

"You ever go on a murder tour?" Bassett asked.

Vivian shook her head. She looked up at the detectives. "I didn't even know what a murder tour was until I read her book."

Bassett and Chen exchanged glances, but said nothing.

"You got family here?" Chen said.

"My sister Hannah. She lives in Oakland."

"You want us to call her, have her come get you?" Bassett said.

Vivian shook her head.

"We'll need her address and phone number," Chen said, pushing a pen and notepad across the table.

Vivian's eyes filled with alarm. "Wait a minute…you're not gonna talk to her about this, are you?"

"It's routine," Bassett said.

"But she had nothing to do with it. Why do you have to talk to her?"

"This is a homicide investigation, Ms. Voss," Chen said. "We're gonna talk to anybody who might have useful information."

"She doesn't have any useful information. The only information she's gonna have is what you tell her."

Chen nodded at the notepad. "Her name, address and phone number, please."

Vivian threw Chen a defiant look. "What if I don't give it to you?"

"You want to be charged with obstruction of justice?" Bassett said.

"You'll go to jail," Chen said. "You sure you want to do that?"

Vivian smiled bitterly. "You guys always win, don't you, no matter how much you wreck people's lives." She jotted down the information, then pushed the notepad back across the table. "Can I go now, or do I need a lawyer?"

"You're free to go," Bassett said, "but we may need to talk to you again." She handed Vivian a business card. "Give us a call if you think of anything that might help."

"You gonna be okay?" Chen asked.

Vivian looked up at him. Her face was pale. "I saw it, okay? So no, I'm not gonna be okay."

Vivian paused on the sidewalk in front of the police station, as if unsure of her next move. The world of the living was everywhere around her, but all she saw was Joanna's bloody corpse playing in her head like a snuff movie she just couldn't turn off.

THREE

THE NIGHT BEFORE.

Vivian looked out the window as the bus pulled into the parking lot. Coit Tower was bathed in light and the lot was filled with folding chairs. A podium had been set up in front of the tower. Joanna had even chartered a tour bus to take attendees to the event. There were banners on both sides of the bus that read:

MURDER TOURS!
Visit San Francisco's Most Notorious Crime Scenes!

The banners were flanked by police chalk outlines of dead bodies.

Joanna had chosen Coit Tower because it was the site of the first attack by the Zebra Killers, who went on a killing spree in the 1970s, taking fourteen lives. A couple out for a walk one evening near the tower was abducted and the woman was sexually assaulted, then nearly decapitated.

The Murder Tour was a radical departure from the period romance novels that had launched Joanna's career and brought her critical and commercial success. But while her earlier novels had been best sellers, her later books sold poorly and were panned as tired and formulaic. Some critics had even suggested that Joanna Rorke had lost her touch.

This new book could not have been more different. Vivian thought it was way more exciting than her older novels, which were set in times long past that Joanna thought was boring. Reviewers called it her strongest work in years. Apparently, readers agreed, because the book had already landed on *The New York Times Best Sellers* list. Vivian had just finished reading *The Murder Tour* and she was looking forward to hearing Joanna read and sign her copy of the book.

The driver opened the door and the passengers began disembarking. He was in his late 40s, with a long, hard face and salt-and-pepper stubble. He was wearing a uniform and a cigarette dangled from his lips. Vivian stepped off the bus and took a seat in the front row. She was wearing a white top with Breton stripes, navy pants, a blazer and ankle boots.

By the time Joanna stepped up to the podium and began to read, every seat in the Coit Tower lot was taken. From her spot in the front row, Vivian laid eyes on a curvy woman in her late 40s or early 50s, with dark eyes and glossy black hair streaked with gray that tumbled to her shoulders. She wore a black sheath dress that accentuated her curves, high heels and a string of pearls. And she read in a husky voice that reminded Vivian of a femme fatale in the old mysteries and thrillers she watched on TV late at night. Most of all, Joanna had a presence that Vivian could feel but not describe.

Joanna took a few questions after the reading. There were the usual ones about where she got her ideas, did she write at night or during the day, did she outline her books, etc. Then a man in the third row asked her why, having written a series of period romance novels, she had decided to write about a serial killer on the loose in San Francisco? Joanna told him that she needed a change of pace, and was looking forward to writing more thrillers set in the present instead of in the past.

She was about to start signing books when a woman in the back raised her hand.

I wanted to ask you if you've ever read a book entitled Tourist Trap?

The woman spoke with a Southern accent. Vivian noticed that the mention of the title seemed to catch Joanna off guard. She gave a tense smile.

No, I've never heard of it and haven't read it.

Of course not. It was never published. I just thought you might have read it in manuscript.

The only manuscripts I read are my own.

That's probably wise.

The exchange puzzled Vivian. Why would someone ask Joanna if she'd read a book that was never published, and why did it unsettle her? Vivian craned her neck to get a look at the woman, but she was sitting in the last row and she was unable to pick her out in the crowd.

After the reading, Vivian waited in line for Joanna to sign her book. It took only a moment, but when Joanna looked up at Vivian and asked her name, Vivian felt as if they were the only two people there. Was that why she had lingered after most of the attendees had boarded the bus? Pretended to take in the view while Joanna chatted with the host of the event and fans who gathered around to congratulate her?

Later, Vivian would tell herself that Joanna must have sensed that she was waiting for her, because she finally excused herself and walked over to Vivian. Just then the bus driver honked the horn twice, a signal that he was about to leave.

"You're going to miss your bus," Joanna said.

"That's okay. I can get a cab in North Beach."

"Perhaps you'd rather have a drink with me?" Joanna said.

FOUR

THEY HUDDLED IN A BOOTH IN THE HOTEL BAR AT THE HYATT REGENCY and when the barmaid came up to the table Joanna ordered two vodka martinis.

Then, after the barmaid moved away, she turned to Vivian and said, "I suppose I should have asked you what you wanted."

Vivian smiled. "It's okay, I like vodka martinis."

"I must have known," Joanna said, in a low, husky voice that made Vivian feel as if she was being seduced.

"Are you wondering why I asked you out for a drink?"

"Yeah, I guess I am," Vivian said, suddenly feeling self-conscious. "Why me, you know?"

"Does it matter?"

"No, I guess not."

"I wanted to, that's all. Is that okay?"

"Yeah, sure. I just wasn't expecting it."

"Sometimes it's best that way," Joanna said.

Their eyes met. Vivian could feel the heat rush into her face as Joanna held her gaze. Then the barmaid returned with their martinis and set them on the table.

Vivian raised her glass in a toast. "Here's to your book. I hope it's a big hit."

"I'll drink to that," Joanna said as they clinked glasses.

"I saw it on *The New York Times* list, so I guess it's already a hit," Vivian said.

Joanna gave a rueful smile. A shadow crossed her face. "Let's hope it stays there." She took another sip and looked at Vivian. "So how'd you like the reading?"

"I thought it was great. I mean, I loved the book…and seeing you read really brought it to life."

"You like to go to readings?"

"Yeah, I do. Hearing an author read, hearing their voices – hearing your voice tonight – it brings a book to life for me. It's not just words on a page. I get to see the person who wrote those words…"

But Joanna wasn't listening. She had turned away from Vivian and was staring at someone. Vivian followed her line of sight and saw a woman sitting at the bar. She was in her late 30s, Vivian guessed, blonde and overweight. She was drinking alone and looking across the room at Joanna. There was a book on the bar in front of her.

"Something wrong?" Vivian said.

But Joanna didn't answer her. Vivian watched as the woman finished her drink and ordered another round. But instead of taking a sip, she slid off the barstool and brought the drink and the book over to the table. Vivian noticed that she was carrying a copy of *The Murder Tour*.

"Well, we meet again, Ms. Rorke," the woman said.

Joanna said nothing. Her face was a mask.

"I didn't get a chance to have you sign my copy of the book," she said, thrusting the book toward Joanna. "Would you mind?"

She spoke with a southern accent. Vivian realized she was the woman at the reading who had asked Joanna about the unpublished manuscript.

"Not at all," Joanna said with a tense smile. She reached in her purse for a pen, then signed the book and handed it back to the woman.

"I sure hope you don't mind that I asked you about *Tourist Trap*," the woman said. "But you know why I did, don't you?"

"What's that supposed to mean?" Joanna said.

The woman gave a knowing smile. "Well, I mean it had to be a coincidence, don't you think? What else could it be if it wasn't a coincidence?"

"I don't know what you're talking about. I think you'd better leave," Joanna said.

"Yes, I suppose I should," the woman said. She threw a glance at Vivian. "You two look so cozy together. But before I go I did want to apologize if I caused you any embarrassment at the reading—"

"You didn't," Joanna said.

"I also wanted to offer my congratulations on *The Murder Tour*. You must be very pleased. I'm sure you'll sell a lot of books." The woman raised the glass in a toast. So...congratulations."

She threw the drink in Joanna's face.

Joanna gasped in shock as the liquor drenched her. Vivian froze, stunned into silence. Others in the bar looked over at Joanna. The bartender rushed over to the table. He grabbed the woman and pushed her toward the exit. "Get out of here! What the hell do you think you're doing?"

"Leaving," the woman said as she shook him off, "that's what I'm doing."

The barmaid came up to the table with towels and handed them to Joanna, who began drying herself.

"I'm very sorry," the bartender said, "this is so embarrassing. Do you want me to call the police? We can have security detain her if you like."

Joanna shook her head. "That won't be necessary."

"Can I offer you another round...on the house?"

Joanna glanced at Vivian. "Have it brought up to my suite."

"Yes, of course," the bartender said, "right away."

Joanna towel-dried her hair in the elevator.

"You don't mind coming up with me, do you? I don't feel like being alone right now."

"Sure, no problem," Vivian said.

The evening had begun with a book reading. Then a woman threw a drink in Joanna's face. Now they were going up to her suite. Everything kept becoming something else and Vivian had no idea what was going to happen next.

"Who was that woman?" she said.

"I don't know, some jealous failure who blames me because she couldn't get published."

"She was the woman from the reading…"

Joanna nodded.

"She acted like she knew you."

Joanna shrugged. "I have no idea who she was. But that's what happens when you get famous. Somebody's always out to get you. I'm just sorry we were interrupted."

But it seemed to Vivian as if this was something more than just a random attack by a disgruntled author. It seemed as if the woman knew Joanna. You don't throw a drink in someone's face for no reason. *But what was the reason? She'll never tell you*, Vivian told herself, *so don't ask. Anyway, it's none of your business.* But the question lingered in Vivian's mind as the elevator doors opened on the top floor and they walked down the hall to Joanna's suite.

The door opened and Vivian walked into a luxury suite that was more than twice the size of her studio apartment. Joanna kicked off her heels and tossed the towel on a chair. Vivian walked over to the window and looked out at the lights of the city. The view took her breath away. It was as if all of San Francisco lay before her.

Joanna came up behind her. "You like the view?" Joanna said.

Vivian nodded. "I love it. I've never seen the city like this."

"I'm glad you like it," Joanna said. Then she pushed her hair up above the nape of her neck and said, "Unzip me, will you? I'm soaking wet."

FIVE

I KNOW WHAT YOU WANT, FLOYD RITTER THINKS AS HE SITS BEHIND THE wheel and watches the tourists board the *Murder Tours* bus. You want to go on the tour. He notices that some of the tourists are clutching copies of Joanna Rorke's new best seller, *The Murder Tour*. Pity what happened to her. Almost more exciting than the book itself, isn't it? But that's why you're here. You want the real thing. Look at you, all lined up, waiting to get on the bus. Just like the tourists who wait to board the cable cars at Powell and Market. You just can't wait to look out the window, can you?

But you don't want to see Coit Tower or the Golden Gate Bridge or Fisherman's Wharf. You want to see the murder sites. There are tours for everything – why not a tour of San Francisco's most gruesome crime scenes? A tour that takes you to the places where the victims were shot or stabbed or strangled or thrown out of a window.

Look, that was where the Zodiac Killer began his killing spree. Oh, and there's the office building where Gian Luigi Ferri killed eight people for no apparent reason. Here we are in Chinatown, the site of the Golden Dragon Massacre that took the lives of five innocent bystanders. Ever heard of The Doodler? He liked to sketch his victims before he stabbed 14 of them to death. Don't miss City Hall, where

Dan White shot and killed Supervisor Harvey Milk and Mayor George Moscone.

There's more, but you get the idea. You want me to show you the crime scenes that made all the headlines. Murder is thrilling. That's why you're here. But what if you were next? Does that ever cross your mind as you look out the window? No, of course not. But it could. So welcome aboard.

You're on the murder tour.

SIX

"You are so busted," Kelli said as Vivian walked into Dumbarton & Dumbarton, the downtown ad agency where she worked as a copywriter. Kelli rocked reception in short skirts, cleavage and a toothy Britney Spears smile. She was the office gossip and lived for dish like it was oxygen. "Where have you been? It's like lunchtime."

Vivian ignored the question. Kelli picked up the phone and tapped a number. "She just got here." She listened for a moment, then put the phone down and looked up at Vivian. "In Donny's office, like now."

Donny Dumbarton was sitting back in his Aeron chair with his hands behind his head and his Nikes up on his desk when Vivian into his office. The walls were decorated with posters of all the ad campaigns he had taken credit for. There was a golf bag filled with clubs by the door. It was branded with a logo that showed a fat white cloud with a yellow thunderbolt and the words *Cloud Cover* wrapped around it.

Donny looked up at Vivian with a pained expression that was supposed to suggest how much it hurt him to push her around. He was stocky, in his 40s, with a goatee and a man bun, and he was the creative director at Dumbarton & Dumbarton. There was only one Dumbarton, but Donny thought repeating the name made the agency sound bigger and more important. But everybody knew it was all about making Donny sound bigger and more important, and referred to the agency as Dumb and Dumber behind his back.

"Where the hell have you been?" Donny said.

"I'm sorry, something came up," Vivian said quietly.

Donny gave her a searching look. "You okay? You don't look too good."

"I think I'm coming down with something," Vivian said.

"Well, don't spread it around here," Donny said. "But whatever you got, get over it, because I need you focused on the *Cloud Cover* business, okay? One hundred and ten percent. Take the afternoon off and be ready tomorrow to come up with some results."

"Got it. Thanks."

"Good. That's what I like to hear."

"You got a tagline yet?"

Vivian shook her head. "I'm working on it."

"Work harder. The client's not gonna wait around forever."

Vivian nodded.

"Okay, that's it, get out of here. Go be creative."

Vivian walked out of Donny's office in a daze. She'd barely heard a word he said. How could he expect her to care about a tagline when she'd walked in on a murder?

She ran into Terry in the corridor. Terry was tall and blonde and gay, and he was Vivian's absolutely best friend. As far as she was concerned, gay men definitely made the best girlfriends. He was the only person who knew everything about her. But he didn't know about Joanna.

"Hey you, where have you been?"

"I have to talk to you," Vivian said.

"Sure, girlfriend, is everything okay?"

Vivian shook her head.

"Okay, c'mon, let's get out of here."

They walked to the Embarcadero and sat on one of the benches facing the bay. It was sunny and bright in the city, with an offshore breeze. The Embarcadero Promenade was a walkway that ran along the bay from Fisherman's Wharf to AT&T Park, home of the San Francisco Giants. You couldn't beat the Embarcadero for waterfront views, and on weekends the promenade was crowded from one end to the other with tourists, cyclists, joggers and parents pushing strollers. But on weekdays it was filled with office workers who spent their lunch hour eating a sandwich or a salad and looking out at the Bay Bridge and the yachts and sailboats dotting the bay.

Terry looked at her. "So what happened?"

Vivian paused. She looked out at the water and for no apparent reason thought about scattering Joanna's ashes.

"I'm really freaked out. I don't even know how to talk about it."

"Just start at the beginning. Tell me what happened."

"Murder. That's what happened."

Terry's jaw dropped, revealing the nicest set of perfectly white teeth. His eyes widened. Vivian noticed that they were blue. He liked to wear different colored contact lenses every day of the week, and he got off on the way people would look at him and do a double take, as if to say, "Weren't your eyes green yesterday?"

"Murder! Who? What are you talking about?"

"I was with her…and now she's dead…and I saw her dead…and I can't stop seeing it." Vivian buried her face in her hands.

Terry put his arm around Vivian and pulled her close.

"I can't believe she's dead…that somebody wanted to kill her," Vivian said. " She looked up at him. "We spent the night together…I don't understand…" She wiped her eyes, then said, "I guess I owe you an explanation."

While Terry listened, Vivian filled him in on her night with Joanna, and her discovery of Joanna's body. When she was finished they both fell silent. Vivian could hear the seagulls calling one to another as they swooped over the bay.

Then Terry said, "I don't know what to say…it must've been awful for you to find her like that."

"I wish I could stop thinking about it, but I can't."

"Do the police have any leads?"

Vivian scoffed. "Yeah, me."

"What are you gonna do now?"

Vivian shrugged. "I'm just gonna go home. Donny Dumb gave me the rest of the day off."

"You want some company?"

Vivian shook her head. "I think I just need to be alone right now."

Terry gave a helpless shrug. "I'm so sorry, girlfriend."

Terry accompanied Vivian to the cable car stop across the street from the agency. Tourists were shooting smartphone pics while they waited for the cable car.

"I want to know what happened to her, Terry."

"I'm sure the police will figure it out."

"Wish I could figure it out."

Terry stared at her. "Are you kidding me? Who are you, Nancy Drew? Just because you read mysteries it doesn't mean you're a detective."

Vivian shrugged it off as if it were a minor detail. She heard the ring of the cable car's bell. "Whatever. I got a right to know what happened. This whole thing's turned my life upside down."

The cable car rattled to a halt and she climbed onboard. Terry watched her with a worried look on his face as the cable car rolled away from the stop and headed up the California Street hill.

SEVEN

Lost in her thoughts as she rode home, Vivian barely heard the rattle of the cable car or the laughter of the tourists hanging off the sides and snapping pics. But then a young couple who looked as if they were on their honeymoon asked Vivian to take their picture.

"Would you mind?" the man said with a hopeful smile as he held out his iPhone.

"Sure, no problem," Vivian said.

The couple posed cheek to cheek and Vivian snapped the pic.

"You guys just get married?"

The couple exchanged shy glances.

"Yeah, how'd you know?" the husband said.

Vivian shrugged. "Just a lucky guess," she said, and handed back the phone.

"Thanks," the woman said. She looked at the pic, then grinned at her husband. "Perfect!"

Tourists, Vivian thought. Where would the city be without them? Then it struck her. "Of course. Tourists," she said to herself.

The cable car reached the Jones Street stop at the top of the hill. Vivian got off and walked across the street to her building. A rumpled, overweight man in his 50s, wearing an ill-fitting blazer and slacks stepped out of a faded Jaguar sedan that was parked at the curb, and approached her.

"Vivian Voss, I presume?" he said in a Cockney accent.

Vivian stopped and looked at him. She noticed he was carrying a notepad.

"Who are you?"

"Freddie Fraser, *San Francisco Sentinel*. I'd like to ask you a few questions."

"You're a reporter?"

"Crime reporter," Freddie said.

"Let me guess: You want to talk to me about Joanna Rorke's murder."

"Right you are. I do."

How did he know about her, Vivian wondered. Had the cops already leaked her name?

"Why should I talk to you?"

"Because I know a bit about crime. Been writing about it for nigh on 30 years now."

"No thanks," she said, "not interested," and headed for the door.

"Hold on a minute," Freddie said, blocking her way.

Vivian narrowed her eyes. "You mind?"

She could see fur balls clinging to his blazer. A fast-food wrapper peeked out of one of the pockets. Freddie pulled out a business card and handed it to Vivian as she opened the door.

"I want your side of the story," Freddie said. "Can't very well get her side, can we? That leaves you. I reckon you want to know what happened. Might help to talk about it."

Vivian smiled politely. She did want to know what happened, but she wasn't about to open up to a stranger on the street. Especially a stranger who happened to be a reporter. She stuffed the card in her purse and went into the building. A black girl in dreads came out of the laundry room with a basket in her arms. She saw Vivian and smiled.

"Hey Viv, what you doing home? You get laid off like me?"

"Hey Shondra," Vivian said. "I took the afternoon off."

"I heard that," Shondra said. "I been takin' 'em all off." She laughed at her joke.

Vivian smiled and pushed the button for the elevator.

"You want to party?" Shondra said.

Vivian shook her head. "Not right now, Shondra, thanks."

Shondra made a face. "You got to alter your reality, girl. You ain't looking too good."

"Yeah, I know," Vivian said as the elevator shuddered to a halt and the doors opened.

Six floors later she walked into her apartment, kicked off her shoes and flopped on the sofa. It felt strange being home in the middle of the day, as if she didn't belong there. Joanna's book was on the coffee table in front of her. She picked it up and opened it. Joanna had signed it on the title page: "To Vivian, with great affection." As Vivian stared at Joanna's signature, it seemed as if it had been written in blood.

She glanced at the bookcase across from her. It was filled with mysteries and thrillers. She had read them all, following sleuths and private eyes and police detectives as they sifted through clues and red herrings and twists and turns to name the killer on the last page. That was what she wanted to do, she told herself. Follow the clues that would lead to Joanna's killer. But who was she kidding? She wasn't a detective or a gumshoe or a private eye. She was just a reader. Maybe Terry was right. It was a mistake to confuse fiction with the real thing. That could lead to even more trouble. But Vivian felt as if she couldn't just sit on the sidelines either. Now that she'd been with Joanna on the last night of her life, how was she supposed to do nothing?

She decided to search for *Tourist Trap* and see what turned up. It wasn't a very original title, Vivian thought, and she assumed that if she searched it on Amazon she would come up with plenty of hits. But there was also a chance that one of those hits would lead her to the author. She assumed there were plenty of online forums and chat rooms where unpublished authors commiserated about their lack of success. Perhaps the author of *Tourist Trap* was one of them.

Vivian fired up her MacBook and began searching. She was right about the use of the title – *Tourist Trap* had been used countless times for dozens of books and movies. But those books and movies had been published and produced; she was searching for the ones that never saw the light of day. She turned next to writers' forums and chat rooms, and surfed through a sea of bitterness and disappointment. It was depressing to read the litanies of failure that appeared in post after post, but Vivian persisted. She was convinced that she had found a way into the investigation, and it thrilled her. Then again, she told herself, it could lead nowhere. She knew from reading mysteries that leads often led to dead ends before the protagonist found the clues that solved the crime. But even if it was a dead end, Vivian was on her way. She was on the case.

Four hours later, her head was pounding and the words on the screen were a blur. She never liked spending long periods of time staring at a computer screen, despite the fact that her job demanded it. She took a break and rubbed her eyes, then stood and walked to the window. Her apartment was on the top floor of a building on Nob Hill, and on a clear day she could catch a glimpse of some of the downtown high rises that shaped the San Francisco skyline. The view wasn't bad, but it didn't compare to the view from Joanna's suite at the Hyatt Regency. But that was one view Vivian never wanted to see again. In her mind's eye the beauty of the city at night had been replaced by an image of Joanna, dead in her bed and drenched with blood.

She went back to the computer and resumed her search. An hour later, buried at the bottom of a web page, Vivian found a recent post that looked promising, even as it stunned her. Because it wasn't really a post, it was an elegy. The poster was the author's wife, and her name was Sylvia Torrey. Vivian stopped cold and stared at her name. The gist of her message was that her husband, Ben Torrey, had written a wonderful mystery novel entitled *Tourist Trap*. The manuscript had been rejected by every agent and publisher he queried. Depressed and despondent over his lack of success, which had apparently gone on for years, he had taken his life. "Beware of what you wish for," his widow wrote, "because it may kill you." Her post was followed by dozen of replies expressing shock and sympathy, but Vivian could not bear to read them.

Torrey's post had knocked the wind out of her. She sat back and closed her eyes. She had searched for an unpublished manuscript and found death instead. First, Joanna and now this unknown author. But was this Sylvia Torrey the same woman who had shown up at Joanna's reading? And was this *Tourist Trap* the same manuscript? And if they were one and the same, what did they have to do with Joanna? Vivian had no idea. But she knew she had found something, even if its meaning was still unclear.

But the fact that she had found what could be a link to the woman at Joanna's reading rushed through Vivian like a shot of adrenaline. Now all she had to do was find the right Sylvia Torrey. But when she typed her name into a search engine, she was dismayed by the sheer number of Sylvia Torreys in the state of California. How could she possibly find the right one? She typed "Ben Torrey" into the search engine and was flooded with another sea of names. Vivian felt as if she was drowning in names that were all the same. She needed to find a way to filter them if she was to narrow them down to the right Ben and Sylvia Torrey.

Vivian had seen the woman up close at the bar. Would she recognize her if she saw her again? She typed "Sylvia Torrey" into the search engine again, then clicked on the "Images" tab. The sea of names was replaced by a sea of faces, none of which resembled the woman Vivian saw in the bar. She exhaled, then closed her laptop. There had to be a better way, she told herself. What would a private investigator do at this stage? How would the amateur detectives in the novels she read follow the clues and find the right Sylvia Torrey?

Vivian had no idea. But it was getting late and she was tired of searching. The late afternoon light was throwing shadows into her apartment. The last 24 hours of her life had been a whirlwind. Her life had been turned upside down and then blown apart, and she'd been left alone to pick up the pieces. Then it occurred to her that the best way to find out if this was the right Sylvia Torrey would be to reach out to her.

All she had to do was join the forum that would allow her to post a reply. Perhaps Sylvia Torrey, if she was the right Sylvia Torrey, would see it and post a reply. Vivian opened her laptop, surfed to the writer's forum, then clicked on the "Register" link at the top of the page, which took her to a registration page. She filled out the forms, then clicked "Submit." A moment later she got a message welcoming her to the forum.

She clicked on Sylvia Torrey's post, read it one more time, then clicked "Reply." Vivian collected her thoughts, then began typing. "If you're the woman who attended Joanna Rorke's reading at Coit Tower last night, then confronted her in the bar and threw a drink in her face, I want to talk to you. I was with her when you did it. If it was you, please reply. It's important."

Vivian reviewed what she'd written, added her email and IM addresses, then clicked "Post." A moment later her reply appeared on the page. Now all she had to do was wait. But what if Torrey was the killer, Vivian wondered. And if she was, would she now come after Vivian because she could identify her? Had Vivian just given the killer a way to find her? Fear gripped her. She froze in its grasp. *Delete the post,* she told herself. *Get rid of it now. Before she has a chance to read it.* Vivian opened her laptop and was about to delete the post when she realized she was overreacting and stopped herself. No, she thought, not yet. You don't know enough to be scared. She threw a glance at mysteries in her bookcase. Those detectives and private eyes didn't run, she thought, even when they were scared. And neither would she.

Her cellphone rang. Vivian glanced at the screen, then took the call.

"Hey girlfriend, you okay?" Terry said.

"Yeah, I'm okay," Vivian said quietly, even if she wasn't.

"You figure out whodunit yet?" Terry said.

Vivian glanced at the web page on her laptop. "Not yet."

"Matt and I are doing happy hour," Terry said, referring to his boyfriend, who did windows for the Saks Fifth Avenue store in Union Square. "Want to join us? You could use a little happiness. Matt wants to hear all about it."

Of course, a total gossip queen *like Matt wanted to hear all about it,*

Vivian thought. It was that kind of story, and after a few rounds it would get even better. But at the moment Vivian was done talking about it. She didn't want sympathy, and she didn't want to explain herself.

"I'll take a rain check," Vivian said. "I just need to hang out tonight."

"You sure? I'm worried about you being alone."

"Yeah, I'm sure."

"OK. Well, we're at The Stud, if you change your mind."

Just what I need right now, Vivian thought. *Drag queens and karaoke at a gay bar south of Market.*

"Have fun, girls, talk to you tomorrow," Vivian said, and ended the call.

She went to the refrigerator, pulled out a bottle of Chardonnay and poured herself a glass. She took a sip, then flopped on the sofa. She grabbed the remote and flipped on the TV. Perhaps she could lose herself in an old movie for a couple of hours. Instead, she landed on a news report about Joanna's murder. A reporter wearing a sports coat and slacks, holding a microphone was standing in front of the Hyatt Regency Hotel. A photo of Joanna Rorke was on the screen. Vivian recognized it as the one that appeared on the inside flap of *The Murder Tour.*

"The literary world got some shocking news this morning," the reporter began, "when best-selling mystery writer Joanna Rorke was found shot to death at the Hyatt Regency hotel. Rorke read from her latest book last night at Coit Tower, and police say she was killed sometime early the next morning. SFPD interviewed a woman who spent the night with Rorke and was apparently the last person to see her alive. The police aren't releasing her name just yet, but when asked if she was a suspect, SFPD said she was a person of interest. As you know, Gwen, 'person of interest' is a term used by law enforcement when identifying someone involved in a criminal investigation who has not been arrested or formally accused of a crime. This is Hal Holland, reporting live from the Hyatt Regency hotel for SF Breaking News. Back to you, Gwen."

"Thanks, Hal," the anchor said. "We'll stay on top of this story as it develops." She looked up at the camera and smiled. "Stay with us. Still ahead: What's up with the fish having sex at Marin's Lagunitas Creek? We'll have a live report."

The station cut to a commercial and Vivian muted the sound. Her heart was pounding. How long would it be before they did release her name, or before somebody leaked it to the media? It was only a matter of time. Then everybody would know. Donny and her coworkers at Dumb & Dumber. Her cheater BF Jake, who would want to hear all about it and might even suggest a threesome. Her sister Hannah, a mom in the suburbs who probably never once in her life thought about having sex with a woman. And then of course there were Vivian's parents, who lived out of state and would conclude that this was what happened to impressionable young women who chose to live in sin city, aka San Francisco.

Vivian wasn't ashamed of what she did; she just didn't exactly want to become famous because of it. But it was too late for that now. Because it wasn't just about sex with a woman. It was about sex with a woman who was murdered. That was the shocking part of the story. It suddenly occurred to Vivian that if she'd still been in the room when the killer entered she might also be dead, and the thought of it made her shudder.

EIGHT

JOANNA BECKONED TO VIVIAN. SHE WAS NAKED AND SMILING AT HER even though a bullet had drilled a hole between her eyes and the bed was a sea of blood. Vivian stared at her, then ran to the door and tried to open it. But the doorknob was missing and there was no way out. She looked back at Joanna, who was still smiling at her.

Kiss me, Joanna said. *Don't you want to kiss me?*

Then Joanna climbed out of bed and walked across the room toward Vivian, leaving bloody footprints on the white carpet. Vivian froze in horror against the wall as Joanna came up to her.

I want you, Joanna said. *I want you forever.*

She put her arms around Vivian and leaned in to kiss her, and at that moment Vivian woke with a gasp, drenched in a cold sweat. She sat bolt upright in bed and gulped air as if she was about to drown. She glanced at the clock on the nightstand and saw it was 3am. Then her iPhone lit up and beeped, alerting her to a text message. She turned on a light and grabbed the phone.

Yes, it's me. What do you want?

Vivian realized that it was Sylvia Torrey, reaching out to her in the middle of the night, and quickly gathered her thoughts and typed a reply.

I want to talk to you.
Who are you?
I was there.
So? Why should I talk to you?
I want to know why you threw a drink in her face.
I had my reasons. Were you her girlfriend?
No.
But you were there.
She bought me a drink.
So what? She's dead.
Please. Let's talk.
Where?
Anywhere you want.

NINE

FREDDIE HAD JUST WALKED INTO THE NEWSROOM AT THE *SAN FRANCISCO Sentinel* when a man in his late 30s with black curly hair and a goatee motioned to him. He wore Dockers and a button-down shirt and tie, and he was standing outside one of the glass offices that ringed the newsroom. Freddie nodded. Here it comes, he thought. He could feel the dread in the pit of his stomach. Was everyone staring at him as he made his way through the sea of desks and cubicles in the crowded newsroom? Or was it his imagination? He was used to it by now, or at least he tried to convince himself that he was used to it.

"You interview the source, Freddie?" the man said as Freddie came up to him.

Freddie looked up at him. "Not yet."

"What happened? You talked to her, right?"

"Yes, well, I tried, Tom, but she turned me down."

Tom scowled. "That's not good enough, Freddie. You know the drill around here."

"Yes, of course…it's just that—"

"No excuses, Freddie. I need you to scoop the story before our competitors do. You dig?"

Freddie nodded. Tom took stock of Freddie as a look of disapproval spread across his face. He plucked the candy wrapper from the pocket of his blazer, then handed it to Freddie.

"Sorry about that," Freddie said, embarrassed.

"You really need to pull yourself together, Freddie. Maybe there's a reason she didn't want to talk to you."

Freddie looked down at his shoes. He could feel his face get hot.

"I want to be on your side here, Freddie, but you gotta meet me halfway. It's been awhile since you broke a story and I need results. If you can't deliver, I can't deliver. You understand?"

Freddie nodded. "Yes, of course."

Tom smiled and patted Freddie on the shoulder.

"Great. Go get 'em."

He turned and walked into his office and closed the door. Freddie made a fist as he crumpled the candy wrapper and walked across the newsroom to his desk.

An older woman with salt-and-pepper hair who sat at a desk across from Freddie looked over at him.

"What was all that about?"

"The usual. Why didn't I get the story?"

"They want us out, Freddie. They just want the young ones now. Dinosaurs like us, we're history."

Freddie said nothing. He shuffled papers on his desk and switched on his computer.

"I heard they're gonna offer buyouts."

Freddie looked at her. "Really?"

The woman nodded. "If they offer me one I'm gonna take it."

Freddie shook his head. "Not me. I want this story. It's a good one, even if he thinks I can't get it."

"You won't have a choice. He'll give it to someone else. And if you don't take the buyout they'll lay you off."

Freddie said nothing. The Joanna Rorke case was a good story. The best one he'd caught in years. He knew it in his bones. A famous writer, murdered in her hotel room. A young woman half her age who'd spent the night with her. If he got it right he could prove to them that he still had the juice, that he still knew how to break a story. But not if they took it away from him. No matter what, he couldn't let that happen. Let the others take buyouts. Freddie Fraser wasn't done. Not by a bloody long shot.

It was so exciting seeing where the murders were committed—it was almost like being there when they happened. Too bad there's not a tour for that!

HARRY PATTERSON, EL CAJON, CA

TEN

Sylvia Torrey agreed to meet Vivian at a Starbucks in the Panhandle, across from Golden Gate Park. Vivian left Donny a message saying that she wasn't feeling well and would be in later that day. She knew he wouldn't be happy about it, but having found Sylvia Torrey, there was no way Vivian was going to let her slip through her hands because of Donny Dumb. She took a quick shower, dressed in slim-fit black jeans, a black leather jacket and boots, then went downstairs to the garage, where she parked her jet-black Triumph Bonneville T100 motorcycle. She unlocked the bike, threw her leg over the frame and started the engine. The sound echoed off the walls as she goosed the throttle. Vivian had bought the bike used from a dealer south of Market on Bryant Street, and despite the fact that it was crazy to ride a motorcycle in the city, she rode it everywhere because nothing else made her feel as free. As she rolled out of the garage and merged into traffic, she estimated that, in rush hour traffic, it could take her close to an hour to get across town.

Forty-five minutes later, she parked across the street from Starbucks. She took off her helmet and shook out her hair, then locked the bike and went inside. She ordered coffee, took a table by the window and waited. The pungent smell of freshly brewed coffee filled the air and Vivian could hear the whine of coffee grinders and the hiss and bubble of cappuccino and espresso machines. Behind the counter, cute young baristas filled orders to the sounds of a Spotify playlist.

She tried to relax, but the image of Joanna's bloody corpse made it impossible. And the fact that her nightmare was followed by a message from the woman who had thrown a drink in Joanna's face created an eerie link between the living and the dead that left her shaken.

Commuters were rushing in and out for coffee as they headed off for work. It occurred to Vivian that if it wasn't for Joanna, she would have been one of them. But instead of sitting at her desk and pounding out copy on deadline, she was waiting to talk to a stranger about murder.

Young people around her age were hanging out, peering at their iPhones, iPads and laptops. They would be there for hours, Vivian knew. Another time, she might've been one of them, lost for hours in a mystery. But she wasn't there to lose herself in someone else's mystery – she was there to solve her own whodunit. The thought of it made her feel like the detective she always dreamed of being. She was on the case, following the clues that would lead to the killer.

As she sipped her coffee, Vivian began to wonder whether Sylvia Torrey would even bother to show up. Ten minutes later, she walked in the door. She was as Vivian remembered her from the bar: late 30s, overweight, blonde hair with roots showing. She was wearing jeans, and a sweatshirt and sneakers, and gave Vivian the impression that she didn't much care how she looked, how she presented herself to the world.

Vivian imagined that Torrey must've recognized her immediately because she walked over to the table and said, "Vivian?"

Vivian nodded. "Thanks for coming."

"I'm gonna get some coffee," Sylvia said, and moved to the counter.

She placed an order, then waited, impatiently drumming her fingers on the counter. Vivian noticed that Sylvia was still wearing a wedding ring. When her coffee was ready she carried it back to the table and sat down. Her face was pale and there was a haggard look in her eyes. Vivian wondered if she was having trouble sleeping and if that was why she messaged her at three in the morning.

Sylvia took a sip of her coffee, then looked at Vivian. "So you want to know why I threw a drink in her face? Is that why we're here?"

"Yes."

"Because she was a thief, that's why."

Vivian's eyes widened. She stared at Sylvia. "Excuse me?"

"Her new book…*The Murder Tour*…"

"What about it?"

"She stole it from my husband."

"What do you mean, stole it?"

"Joanna taught an online writing seminar one summer, asked students to send her their manuscripts and she would critique them. But she didn't just critique Ben's book, she stole it."

"I don't understand…" Vivian said, shocked to hear Joanna accused of plagiarism.

Sylvia's face tightened. She looked sharply at Vivian. "It's the same fucking story, okay? The exact same story. She just changed the title. She needed a hit so she stole it. Nobody wanted Ben's book, he kept sending it out and everybody kept rejecting it. When he saw her book come out it pushed him over the edge. Killed him. He committed suicide one day while I was at work."

"I'm sorry," Vivian said.

Sylvia looked sharply at Vivian. "What the hell you sorry for? You didn't know him. He wasn't your husband."

"When you asked her at the reading about *Tourist Trap*, was that the book?"

"Yeah, that was it."

Sylvia reached into her bag and pulled out a flask. She opened it and spiked her coffee. She looked up at Vivian.

"You want some?"

Vivian shook her head. "Thanks, it's a little early for me."

Sylvia smiled bitterly. "Used to be for me too, but not anymore." She sipped her coffee, then capped the flask and put it back in her bag. "So how come she bought you a drink?"

"I don't know, exactly. I just went to her reading and one thing led to another."

"Just like that, huh?"

Vivian nodded, embarrassed.

"You sorry she's dead?" Sylvia said.

"Well, yeah—"

"I'm not. The bitch had it coming."

"You think she deserved to die?"

Sylvia's face hardened. "Did my husband deserve to die?" She drained her cup, then reached in her bag. Vivian thought she was pulling out the flask, but instead she pulled out a flash drive and pushed it across the table. "See for yourself if she didn't steal his book." Then she abruptly stood and walked to the door.

Vivian jumped to her feet. "Wait!"

Sylvia ignored her and walked out the door. Vivian pocketed the flash drive and went out after her.

"Sylvia!" she shouted.

Vivian ran out after her and saw Torrey climb into a silver Nissan Sentra. As she drove away, Vivian memorized the license plate.

ELEVEN

DID SHE DO IT?

Vivian pondered the question as she sat on her bike outside Starbucks.

Did I just have coffee with a killer?

Vivian tried to picture Sylvia slipping into Joanna's room and pointing a gun at her head and pulling the trigger. But the real thing was always hard to imagine. Sylvia hated Joanna, that much was clear. Did she hate her enough to kill her? Vivian had no idea. Clearly she had motive. Joanna deserved to die for stealing her husband's book and apparently driving him to suicide. Sylvia had passed judgment on Joanna and declared her guilty of capital crimes – but was she willing to carry out the death sentence? Vivian realized the police needed to know. She had told them about the woman who had thrown a drink in Joanna's face and now Vivian knew who she was. They would certainly consider Sylvia Torrey a suspect in Joanna's murder.

Vivian fumbled in her bag for the business cards Bassett and Chen had given her when they interviewed her. Bassett's card tumbled out, along with Freddie Fraser's business card. She reached for her phone and was about to tap Bassett's number when she realized that she couldn't tell Bassett about her coffee date with Sylvia Torrey without telling her how she'd found her. And that would mean acknowledging that she was conducting her own investigation on the down low. There would be consequences for her actions. Vivian assumed that Bassett and Chen would be only too happy to usher her into a windowless interrogation room and explain it all to her. Vivian decided that for now she would keep what she knew to herself.

Then she thought of Laura Neville, the woman who'd texted Joanna to remind her of their date for breakfast at the hotel. If Sylvia hated Joanna, what did Neville think of her? She must've considered Joanna a friend, otherwise why have breakfast with her? Vivian decided she wanted to talk to her. She was the only other lead Vivian had, besides Sylvia, and as a friend she would provide another perspective on Joanna, one that might prove helpful to the investigation.

Vivian had no idea whether the police knew about Neville, but it was possible that she had contacted the police on her own once she learned of Joanna's death. But even if they had interviewed her, Vivian knew that the police would not divulge the details of that interview, or enable Vivian to interview Neville herself. She needed to find another way to reach her. Her eyes fell on Freddie Fraser's business card. She put on her helmet, started the engine and headed back across town.

TWELVE

THE SAN FRANCISCO SENTINEL BUILDING WAS SOUTH OF MARKET ON Mission Street. Vivian circled the block several times until she found the right parking space. Then she locked the bike, fed the meter and went into the lobby. When the receptionist looked up at her, she asked for Freddie Fraser.

"Do you have an appointment?" the receptionist said.

"Tell him it's Vivian Voss."

Five minutes later Freddie Fraser ambled into the lobby, notepad in his hand, and smiled at Vivian. He was wearing the same ill-fitting blazer and slacks as before, though he'd apparently removed the fast-food wrapper that was peeking out of one of his pockets. Vivian assumed he'd finished eating whatever was in it.

"Well, this is a pleasant surprise," Freddie said as he came up to Vivian. "Changed your mind, did you?"

Vivian shrugged. "Maybe. I thought we could talk."

"Excellent." Freddie glanced at his watch, then looked up at Vivian. "Fancy a bite to eat?"

"Eat?" Vivian said with a wan smile. A feeling of dread came over her as she remembered the fast-food wrapper.

"You do eat, don't you?"

"Well, yeah, sure...I just wasn't expecting—"

"There's a lovely place just down the street. We can talk there."

"Sure," Vivian said, forcing a polite smile.

Freddie swiveled to the receptionist. "Cheerio, out to lunch, love," he said with a wave. Then he turned and held the door open for Vivian. "Shall we?"

"Did you know her?" Freddie asked as they walked down Mission Street.

"Joanna Rorke?" Vivian said.

Freddie nodded.

Vivian shook her head. "I met her at the reading."

"You like to go to readings, do you?"

Vivian gave a rueful smile. "I used to."

"Yes, quite." Freddie said. Then he looked up and smiled. "Ah, here we are."

Vivian's heart sank as Freddie escorted her into a fast-food shack. The colorful sign out front said BIGGA BURGER in fat red letters and featured a cartoon illustration of a giant hamburger from outer space hovering over the city.

"You eat here?" Vivian said in disbelief.

"Nearly every day," Freddie said as they stepped inside. "Though I don't usually have such lovely company." He smiled at Vivian, then pointed to a booth by the window. "Shall we sit there?"

Freddie led Vivian to the booth and they sat down. The air was thick with fast-food grease. Vivian felt as if she could scarcely breathe. A tiny Asian waitress appeared and dropped two laminated, ketchup-stained menus on the table. "You got date, Freddie?" she said, giving Vivian the once-over.

"Business," Freddie said with a chuckle.

The waitress was not persuaded. "She too skinny for you," she said, shaking her head as she moved away from the table.

Vivian was mortified. She wanted to crawl under the table, but was afraid of what she might find there. What had seemed like a good idea at the time seemed now to have been a disastrous miscalculation.

"Don't mind her," Freddie said. "They're always trying to fix me up." He grinned. "I tell 'em I'm already married to me cats." His eyes dropped to the menu. "I think it's the BIGGA bacon cheeseburger for me today." He set the menu aside and looked at Vivian. "What about you, love?"

"Do they have salads?" Vivian said.

Freddie was stumped. He looked up at her as if she'd asked for a foreign object that didn't actually exist. "Salads?"

"You know, with lettuce and tomato and stuff…"

"Can't say as I've ever seen one here, but I suppose they could whip one up for you."

He motioned to the waitress. When she came over to the table Freddie ordered his burger, along with a Coke and a supersize order of fries.

The waitress jotted down the order, then nodded at Vivian. "What she want?"

"I'll have a salad, please," Vivian said.

The waitress looked at her, then at Freddie. "What she say?"

"She said she'd like a salad."

The waitress muttered to herself as she jotted down Vivian's order, then moved away from the table.

"That's what I like about this place," Freddie said, "the personal touch."

"So what do you want to know?" Vivian said. "I've already talked to the police."

"Quite. But talking to the police can be a bit dodgy for most people, as it makes them feel they're being judged on everything they say."

Vivian nodded. "Yeah, you're right about that."

"I have no interest in judging you, but there's always the story behind the story, you see. That's what I'm interested in."

Vivian looked at Freddie. "What do you mean, the story behind the story?"

"Well, it's a bit juicy, isn't it, you and this woman?"

Vivian stiffened. "What are you, a perv, Freddie?"

Freddie chuckled. "No, but my readers might be."

Vivian frowned. "Maybe this isn't such a good idea—"

Freddie leaned in toward Vivian, an earnest look on his face. "Look, Vivian, it's not every day that a young woman like yourself goes to a book reading and then shags the author—"

Vivian's eyes widened. "Excuse me?"

"…who then turns up dead the next morning. From what I understand, you found the body."

Vivian looked around to see if anyone had heard Freddie, then lowered her voice and said, "How'd you know I…?"

"Shagged the author?"

Vivian nodded as the color rushed into her face. "And how'd you know I found the body?"

"I'm a crime reporter, love, which means I talk to the police and they talk to me."

"That's what I wanted to talk to you about," Vivian said.

Freddie looked up at her and waited for the rest of it.

"Help me figure out what happened and I'll tell you everything you want to know."

Freddie stared at Vivian, a surprised look on his face. "Say what?"

"That's the story you want, isn't it? My night with Joanna? All the juicy details?"

The waitress returned with their orders. She set Freddie's cheeseburger and fries down first. Then, in what seemed like an afterthought, she gave Vivian a soup bowl with iceberg lettuce and sliced tomatoes swimming in Thousand Island dressing.

Freddie beamed as he looked at his burger and fries. He unfolded his napkin and stuffed it into his shirt collar.

"Well, dig in, as you Yanks like to say." He picked up his bacon burger with both hands and bit into it. A shot of grease spurted out. It arced across the table, nearly hitting Vivian. More grease ran down Freddie's hands and dripped onto the napkin. He wiped his mouth and looked at Vivian, who was picking at her salad. "You were saying?"

Vivian looked up at him. "What if I told you I might know who killed her?"

Freddie stopped in mid-bite. His eyes widened. He put his burger down and stared at Vivian.

"I had coffee with her this morning," Vivian said.

"I'm listening," Freddie said as he wiped his hands on the napkin.

He ignored his burger and began taking notes as Vivian filled him in on Sylvia Torrey and *Tourist Trap*, and how she found her through a writer's forum. Then she told him about the question she had asked at the reading, the drink she threw in Joanna's face and the accusation she made when Vivian met her for coffee.

Freddie nodded, impressed. "You're quite the little detective, aren't you? Did you tell the police?"

Vivian shook her head.

"Why not?"

"I didn't think they'd like the idea of me messing around with the case."

"Yes, you're quite right about that. You start mucking about in police business you'll be charged with interfering with an investigation." Freddie paused. "Why the devil is it so damn bloody important to you?"

"I was there. I was with her, okay? I did something with Joanna that I've never done with anyone else. The night I spent with her... nothing like that ever happened to me before...I don't know how to explain it...it was like I became somebody I've never been before... and to be the last person who saw her alive before she was killed...and then to find her dead...I just can't let it go. I need to know." Vivian looked up at Freddie. "Just like you need to know."

Vivian read the look on Freddie's face and saw she had not persuaded him. She leaned in and said, "This is bigger than just me and Joanna, okay? It's about who killed her and why, and you could get the scoop."

"Well, I'd love the scoop, but is it worth the risk? Have you thought about that?"

"I want to know what happened. Just like in mysteries, they always figure out whodunit. All my life I've been reading about how private eyes and detectives solved cases, and the more I read the more I wanted to do it myself. Not just to read about it, but to actually *do* it, to actually solve a case."

Freddie gave a weary shrug. "Those are books, love, not real life. The two got nothing to do with each other. Anyway, I'm a reporter, not a detective."

"You said you've been writing about crime for 30 years."

Freddie nodded. "Yes, I have. Murder and mayhem, that's been me lot."

"So you probably know as much about murder as the police or anybody else."

"I know a bit, I suppose. But it's not the same—"

"Teach me," Vivian said, cutting him off.

"Teach you what, love?"

"Why people kill people. Why somebody killed Joanna Rorke. If it wasn't Sylvia Torrey, then who was it? I think we can help each other. I tell you what I know and together we find out what happened to Joanna. You want the story, don't you?"

"Yes, but I don't want to go to jail for it." Freddie paused. "You must be daft," he gave a rueful smile. "I must be daft as well."

"So we have a deal?" Vivian said .

"We?"

"We're partners, aren't we?"

Freddie sighed. "Yes, I'll remember that when they put the cuffs on us."

THIRTEEN

FREDDIE HAD NOT EXPECTED VIVIAN TO REACH OUT TO HIM. THAT HAD come as a complete surprise. He was convinced she would never agree to an interview, which meant he would never get the story, and as a result he would be pressured to take a buyout and leave the paper. But that was the last thing he wanted to do. He would leave on his own terms when the time came, not because he was being shown the door. But Vivian had made sure that wasn't going to happen anytime soon. He knew he was taking a chance with her. She was playing detective in her imagination, but this was real life and real murder.

Still, she was the heart of the story. No matter what the risk, it was too good to pass up. He knew that while this could put him back on top, it could also land him in jail. But he'd never had an opportunity quite like this one. Not even when he worked the crime beat for the Fleet Street rags in London years ago. This was a chance to not just report the story, but also to solve the crime behind the story. What would Tom think of that? What would any of them think when the story broke? This was front-page news, above the fold.

Freddie was standing outside the building, puffing on a cigarette, when he saw Tom approach the entrance, apparently on his way back from lunch. A female reporter was tagging along with him. Freddie had seen her around the newsroom, but had never worked with her. She was in her 20s at the most, fresh out of journalism school and, like most of the younger reporters on the paper, eager and hungry for a scoop. Wouldn't she love the story I've got in my pocket, Freddie thought. Then he remembered that if he wasn't careful Tom might just give it to her.

"Hey Freddie," Tom said. He nodded at the cigarette. "Still haven't given it up, huh?"

Freddie stubbed out the cigarette and put the butt in his pocket. "I'm working on it."

"You gotta work harder, Freddie. Set an example."

"Yes, of course."

"Got any news for me?"

"I do as a matter of fact," Freddie said. He paused for effect, then said, "I interviewed my source. Just had lunch with her." He stopped there, leaving out the fact that he and Vivian had agreed to work on the case together. There was no need for Tom to know more than was absolutely necessary.

"That's great," Tom said. "Glad to hear it." He turned to the young reporter. "Freddie's working on the Joanna Rorke story."

"Wow," she said, her eyes glittering with envy. "Let me know if you need any help."

"Thanks, but I think I've got the hang of it."

"Lisa could be a great resource for you, Freddie. You might want to keep her in mind."

Freddie smiled politely as Tom and Lisa walked into the building. Then he pulled the butt out of his pocket, re-lit it and took a deep and defiant drag. When he got back to his desk he reviewed the notes he'd jotted down during his lunch with Vivian. He spotted Laura Neville's name and decided that the woman who was planning to have breakfast with the victim was a good place to start. But first he had to find her. He picked up the phone, punched in a number, then waited.

"Hello, love, Freddie Fraser here." He listened for a moment, then smiled and said, "Lovely. You?"

Freddie made small talk for a few minutes, then got down to business. He needed contact information for a certain Laura Neville, and would she be so kind as to help him out.

"Freddie, you know I'm not supposed to give out that kind of information. This is the DMV, for God's sake."

"Yes, I know, love, but I'm on deadline and I really need to speak to her."

"You're always on deadline."

"Yes, quite."

Freddie heard the woman on the other end sigh.

"What was her name again?

Freddie smiled. "Laura Neville. N-E-V-I-L-L-E."

FOURTEEN

By the time Vivian got home she was filled with anticipation. Because now, instead of living vicariously through the lives of fictional characters, she was living her own *real life* crime drama. And if she and Freddie did manage to solve Joanna's murder, it would be as thrilling a tale as any she'd ever read. Even better because it would be true.

She understood they were taking a chance that could land them both in jail or worse, but she was in her late 20s now. Before the year was out she would turn 29. Three decades of her life had flashed by, like the pages she turned reading late into the night. If she didn't start writing her own story now, then when?

She was about to put the bike in the garage when a Honda Civic with a boy racer exhaust system roared around the corner and pulled up in front of her building. Vivian turned and glanced at the car.

"Hey, Viv!" the driver shouted over the sound of hip hop booming out of the car's sound system. The window was down on the passenger side and her ex-BF Jake was behind the wheel. He was in his late 20s, and he was wearing a baseball cap, jeans and sunglasses. He flashed that TV star smile that had always worked for him.

"Great. Just what I need," Vivian muttered to herself.

"I've been calling you, babe, you get my messages?"

"We broke up, Jake, remember?" She stepped to the front door of her building.

"Can I come up?" Jake said.

Vivian turned and looked at him. "Why, so we can be boyfriend and girlfriend again?"

"Come on, it was only one time, what's the big deal?"

"Seriously, Jake? Am I supposed to be grateful that it was only one time?" Vivian shook her head and opened the garage door.

"You hear about that writer who got killed?"

Vivian paused as the words slammed into her. *The writer who got killed.* Keep walking, she told herself. It'll only get worse if you don't. Jake would talk his way into her apartment and before long into her pants. She rode the bike into the garage and closed the door behind her.

Her intercom buzzed the moment she walked into her apartment. She glanced at it and scowled.

"Go away, Jake," she muttered. Then she walked over to the intercom and pressed the button. "What?" she said.

"Are you some kind of lesbian now?" a woman said.

Vivian rolled her eyes and sighed.

"Hannah," she said. "Come up."

FIFTEEN

THE DOORBELL RANG. VIVIAN TOOK A DEEP BREATH, THEN WENT TO THE door and opened it. Hannah, a sandy-haired woman who looked about five years older than Vivian was standing there. She was wearing sunglasses, a UC Berkeley sweatshirt and jeans. Two boys were standing next to her. They chased each other into Vivian's apartment the moment the door opened.

"The police came to the house," Hannah said. "What the fuck is going on?"

"Hi, sis," Vivian said.

"They said you were with some woman who got murdered," Hannah said as she stepped into the apartment and closed the door. "They said you found the body."

Vivian nodded as Joanna flashed before her eyes.

"That must've been awful for you," Hannah said.

"Yeah, it was."

The boys were doing laps around the coffee table. Vivian tensed as she waited for them to break something in her perfectly neat apartment.

"Are you a lesbian now?"

"Oh for God's sake, Hannah," Vivian said as she flopped back on the sofa.

"Why didn't you tell me you were a lesbian?" Hannah said. "Not that there's anything wrong with being a lesbian, I just wish you'd told me so I didn't have to find out from the cops."

"I'm not a lesbian, okay?"

Hannah sat down next to her. "You sure?"

Vivian rolled her eyes.

"You smell like a cheeseburger," Hannah said.

"Don't remind me," Vivian said.

"I thought you didn't like cheeseburgers."

"It's a long story," Vivian said. She nodded at the boys, who were pretending they were police sirens. "Could you get 'em to turn it down before I get evicted?"

"Sure, no problem," Hannah said. Then she let out a whistle that nearly punctured Vivian's eardrums. The boys stopped dead in their tracks. "Say hello to Aunt Viv," Hannah said.

"Hi, Aunt Viv," the boys said in unison. Then they turned the sirens back on.

"Stop!" Hannah shouted. "You're giving me a headache."

The boys stopped cold and stared at their mother. "Can we watch TV?" one of them said..

"Sure, knock yourself out," Vivian said, handing them the remote. "Just keep it down."

The boys flopped on the floor near the sofa and started switching channels. Out of the corner of her eye, Vivian saw daytime TV flashing on the screen.

Hannah turned to her. "Okay, start at the beginning," she said.

Vivian sighed, then filled Hannah in on her night with Joanna. She had already been through it with the police, and Terry, and retelling it now to Hannah, now that it was public knowledge, made her feel sordid.

"I did it once with a girl," Hannah said after Vivian was finished.

Vivian's eyes widened. "You?" she said, surprised.

Hannah nodded. "Back in college. Me and my roommate."

"How was it?"

Hannah shrugged. "It was okay. Kinda like making love to yourself, you know what I mean? Same body parts. I felt like we were mirror images of each other. I missed the penetration part, even if that's not always what it's cracked up to be." She looked at Vivian closely. "So what are you gonna do now?" she said, changing the subject.

Vivian paused. Hannah didn't need to know that what she wanted to do was find out who killed Joanna and why. "I don't know," she said.

"You want to come stay with us until it blows over?"

Vivian made a face. She nodded at the boys.

Hannah followed her gaze, and said, "Trust me. You get used to it."

Vivian shook her head. "Thanks, sis, but I don't want to get used to it."

Hannah gave her sister a long look. "So what are you gonna be, some kind of semi-lesbian walking the streets alone?"

Vivian's face showed shock as she stared at her sister. Then she burst out laughing. Hannah joined her, and for the moment it was fun just to laugh together. But then it was time to round up the boys and head for home across the Bay Bridge before the traffic got any worse and gridlock turned the bridge into a parking lot.

"Just think about it, okay?" Hannah said as she embraced her sister.

"Okay, I'll think about it," Vivian said.

"Good."

Vivian watched as Hannah climbed in behind the wheel of her enormous SUV and started the engine. She honked the horn, the boys waved out the windows, then they were gone. Vivian remained on the sidewalk in front of her building. She was, depending on who you talked to, a copywriter, a person of interest or a semi-lesbian. These thoughts tumbled through Vivian's mind as a *Murder Tours* bus rolled down California Street. It was black and white with police chalk outlines on the side. Just like the bus she had taken to Joanna's reading at Coit Tower.

Was it the same bus, she wondered, *or did they have a fleet of buses?* Vivian got her answer when she caught a glimpse of the driver and saw it was the same man who was driving the bus the night of Joanna's reading at Coit Tower: late 40s, long, hard face, salt-and-pepper stubble. A cigarette dangled from his lips. Was it her imagination, or did he seem to slow down and stare at her as he passed her building? *What does he know about Joanna?* Vivian wondered. *What does he know about me?*

SIXTEEN

FLOYD RITTER WHEELS THE *MURDER TOURS* BUS INTO A PARKING SPACE across the street from the Hyatt Regency. He smiles grimly as he looks out at the entrance to the hotel, which is ringed with yellow crime scene tape. Uniformed police officers stand guard by the doors. He glances in the rearview at his passengers. Every seat is taken. *Peeping Toms and voyeurs,* Ritter thinks, *wanting the thrill of murder without having to pull the trigger. If only you knew what it was really like to kill,* Ritter thinks. He shuts off the engine and reaches for the microphone, then stands and faces the passengers.

"Okay, listen up, folks."

The passengers look up at him with expectant faces. This is the good part, Ritter imagines they're thinking. This is why we're here. They've looked out at the window and seen the police and the entrance ringed with tape. Something happened here. Was it murder?

"My name's Floyd..."

"Hi Floyd," the passengers say in unison, as if they're at an AA meeting.

"I'd like to thank you all for joining me today, and I hope you enjoy the tour. When it comes to murder, San Francisco's got something for everybody."

A nervous titter runs through the passengers.

"You know, most of the time we visit crime scenes where terrible murders were committed in the past. But today I'm adding an extra stop on the tour. So in case you're wondering why we're parked in front of the Hyatt Regency, it's because somebody famous was murdered here just the other day. This one's fresh," Ritter says with a cold smile. He pauses, then says, "Anybody know who was killed here?"

"Joanna Rorke," one of the passengers shouts.

"You're right," Ritter says. "Who else knows Joanna Rorke was murdered here?"

Hands shoot up from one end of the bus to the other.

"I was at her reading," a middle-aged man in the third row says.

"So was I," says a mother of three in the first row.

"You're lucky," Ritter says, "You saw her just before she was killed, while she was still warm. Kind of exciting, isn't it?"

Ritter sees the glitter in their eyes as they contemplate what it was like to see Joanna Rorke moments before she stopped breathing.

"How was she killed?" a soldier in uniform asks.

"Shot to death in her room at point-blank range," Ritter says.

A murmur runs through the passengers.

The soldier persists. "How do you think it happened?"

Floyd shrugs. "Can't say, I wasn't there."

"Got any ideas?'

"Well, like I said, I wasn't there, but I can tell you how I think it happened. Is that what you want to hear?"

"Yeah, tell us all about it!" a passenger shouts as the rest of the passengers applaud.

"Well, the way I figure it," Ritter begins, "she was still in bed when the killer walked into her room."

"How'd he or she get into the room?"

"Probably managed to steal a passkey from a maid or bellboy."

"Then what happened?"

"The killer would have had to cover the sound of the gunshot, so he or she probably flipped the TV on and turned up the volume so it was really loud. The sound probably woke her up, but she was still half-asleep and she probably couldn't figure out why the TV was on or why it was so loud."

"I'll bet the guests in the room next door started pounding on the walls," a young wife offers.

"Yeah, or maybe they called the front desk to complain," her husband adds.

"You're right," Ritter says. "Which meant the killer didn't have much time. So he or she probably just shot her as she started to get out of bed, then turned the TV down and slipped out of the room."

"She must've been scared when she saw the gun," the soldier says.

Ritter nods. "Last thing she ever saw."

"Boy, you're not just a bus driver, you're a storyteller, aren't you, Floyd?" the middle-age man says.

Ritter gives a cold smile. "You learn a lot about murder driving the bus."

"Can we see her room?" the mother of three asks.

Ritter smiles and shakes her head. "Sorry." He nods at the police officers. "The cops won't let us in. But feel free to get off the bus and take pictures of the hotel. A famous murder happened here, and you'll want to tell your friends and neighbors all about it when you get back home."

Ritter sits down and opens the door. The passengers clamber off the bus clutching their cameras and iPhones. He watches them with the contempt he reserves for those who like to watch. Then he reaches for his cell phone and punches in a number.

"Where are you?" he says.

"I'm just leaving. I have to go to work."

"You're avoiding me," Ritter says

"It's just not a good time for me."

"Why?"

"You know why."

"No, I don't."

"Can we talk about this some other time?"

"That's what you always say."

"I'm sorry."

"Yeah, sure you are," Ritter says. "You're always sorry, aren't you?"

"I just lost my husband."

"That didn't stop you when he was alive. Why now that he's dead?"

"I don't know why, it just feels different now. Maybe I just need some time."

"You're not scared, are you?"

"Why? Should I be?"

"No, of course not."

"I'm just on edge."

"I want to see you."

"Are you sure that's a good idea?"

"Tonight, after work," Ritter says, as the tourists shuffle back onto the bus.

SEVENTEEN

THE PHONE FEELS SLIPPERY IN HER HAND. SYLVIA FINISHES DRESSING AND looks at herself in the mirror. She's wearing her Safeway uniform. She hates the way it looks on her, but she has no choice. She has to wear it if she wants to keep her job. Ben said she'd never have to work again, that he'd take care of her. That everything they dreamed about would come true. The book is going to sell, he told her. Just wait and see. Then he gassed himself in the car. She found him when she got home from work. *He took care of himself,* Sylvia thinks. *That's what people who commit suicide always do – they take care of themselves.*

Now Floyd wants to see her. He likes to see her after work because he wants to watch her take off her uniform. He always likes that part. *I like it too,* Sylvia thinks, *more than I should. But what if he finds out what happened? What made them think they could get away with it? Joanna Rorke thought she could get away with it, and look what happened to her. Now that girl is asking questions. What was her name? Vivian, yes, Vivian. She'll look at what's on the flash drive and see that Joanna got what was coming to her.* But it doesn't make Sylvia feel any better. *The dead move on,* she thinks, *but you're still the same.*

What if I just went away, Sylvia thinks. *Just disappeared.* She could get away with it. People vanish all the time. She could become a missing person, join all the other missing persons who are never heard from again. She could do it right now, this morning. Just get in the car and drive away. She goes into the closet and pulls out a suitcase. She puts it on the bed and opens it. She stares at the emptiness and thinks about how Ben promised her that they would travel, go wherever she wanted for as long as she wanted. But he was the only one who went anywhere, and it was a one-way trip.

Sylvia opens a dresser drawer and starts pulling out her things and throwing them into the suitcase. She goes into the closet and looks at her wardrobe, then pulls clothes off the hangers and puts them on the bed. But almost immediately she stops and closes the suitcase. *Who am I kidding?* she thinks. He would never let her get away. Ben had to kill himself to get away. What was she supposed to do, gas herself in her car because it was the only way to escape? That was Ben's solution and look where it got him. She remembers that the medical examiner found drugs in Ben's system, tranquilizers, he told her, to help him relax. Why, she asked him, so he could get up his nerve to die? She feels the anger building inside her, as if she's about to explode with rage.

She opens the drawer on the nightstand next to the bed and takes out the framed photographs of her and Ben that she had taken down after his death because she could not bear to look at them. She put them in a drawer but she still takes them out and looks at them anyway. *No more*, she tells herself. She has to get away from the past if she's to have any kind of future. She takes the photographs out of the frames and puts them in a stack on the bed next to her. As her eyes fill with tears, she begins tearing them to pieces.

Then she sees a flash drive in the bottom of the drawer. *Which one is it?* Sylvia wonders. Is it the one she gave Vivian or the other one? She wipes her eyes, then inserts the flash drive into her laptop. She waits until the file appears on her desktop, then opens it. Her face goes white as she stares at the title page.

EIGHTEEN

LAURA NEVILLE LIVED IN AN UPSCALE CONDO THAT WAS WITHIN walking distance of the Broadway Plaza shopping mall, Walnut Creek's main attraction.

"All a bit tidy, isn't it," Freddie said as he pulled into a parking space, then looked out at the manicured lawns.

Vivian shrugged. The suburbs all looked the same to her, and she never much liked shopping in malls.

"She knows, right?" Vivian said.

"About Joanna?"

Vivian nodded.

"She must know, it's been all over the news."

"What do we tell her about us?"

"Us?"

"How we found out about her."

"You lie, love."

Vivian looked at him. "What do you mean?"

"You make something up."

"Like what?"

"Tell her Joanna mentioned she was going to have breakfast with her. You say what you need to say to get the story."

"Whether it's true or not?"

Freddie scoffed. "Nobody cares about the truth, love. They only care about what they want to believe."

"What does Laura Neville want to believe?"

"That we cared about Joanna Rorke and were saddened by her death."

"Excuse me, you didn't even know her."

"Yes, but you did, love, biblically speaking."

Freddie opened the door and got out of the car. Vivian followed suit, happy to get out of the car, which reeked of cigarettes. They went up to the door and rang the doorbell. Moments later, a middle-aged woman with a face tight enough to have been lifted more than once, opened the door.

"Yes?"

Vivian and Freddie exchanged glances, then Vivian said, "Ms. Neville?"

"Yes, I'm Laura Neville. What's this about?"

"It's about Joanna Rorke," Freddie said.

Neville looked stricken. "Joanna! Did you know her?"

"I understand you were a friend," Vivian said.

"Yes, that's true."

"That's what we wanted to talk to you about," Freddie said.

"Who are you?" Neville said.

"My name's Vivian Voss."

"Freddie Fraser, *San Francisco Sentinel*."

Neville looked sharply at Freddie. "You're a reporter?"

Freddie nodded.

"Are you writing a story about her?"

Freddie nodded. "Yes, about the case."

Neville looked at Vivian. "Are you a reporter too?"

Vivian and Freddie exchanged glances, then Freddie jumped in to save her.

"She's my assistant," he said.

"May we come in?" Vivian said.

"Yes, all right," Neville said, and stepped aside as Vivian and Freddie stepped into the house and went into the living room. She motioned to the sofa. "Please, sit down."

Vivian and Freddie walked over to the sofa and sat down. Neville settled into one of the chairs facing the sofa. The décor was very Pottery Barn and reminded Vivian of her sister Hannah's house.

"Did you know Joanna?" Neville said.

"I went to her reading," Vivian said, conveniently leaving out the fact that she knew much more than that.

"I wanted to go, but I couldn't make it. I told her I'd go to the next one, and then…" Her voice trailed off and the room fell silent as a tomb. Then she looked up at Vivian and said, "But how did you know about me?"

"I had a drink with her after the reading and she told me she was having breakfast with you."

"Yes," Neville said. "I texted her but I never heard back from her." She paused as her face seemed to collapse. "Then I saw it on the news."

"Forgive me for asking, but did she have any enemies?" Freddie said.

"Why do you ask?"

"There was a woman at the reading who asked Joanna if she'd read a book that wasn't published," Vivian said. "Then, when we were in the bar she threw a drink in Joanna's face."

A sad smile softened Neville's face. "Was it about *Tourist Trap*?"

Vivian looked at her. "Yes. How did you know?"

"I'd heard the rumors, I even asked Joanna about them."

"What kind of rumors?" Freddie said.

"Oh, that she'd lost her touch and that the only reason the new book was such a success was because she'd plagiarized it."

"Did you ask her about the rumors?" Vivian said.

"Oh sure, but she always denied them and said people were jealous because she'd made a comeback."

"Did you believe the rumors?" Freddie said.

Neville shrugged. "I don't know. Joanna was desperate for a hit and the book was such a change for her, so different from what she'd written before. I think that and the rumors made people wonder." She shook her head sadly. "I suppose it doesn't matter now. The rumors can't hurt her anymore."

"Quite," Freddie said quietly.

"Do you think she killed her? The woman who threw a drink in her face?"

Vivian and Freddie looked from one to another.

"It's possible," Vivian said. "She was angry enough. Does the name Sylvia Torrey mean anything to you?"

Neville thought about it for a moment, then shook her head.

"No, it doesn't."

"What about Ben Torrey?"

"Sorry, no. Never heard of him either."

"Sylvia's the woman who threw the drink in Joanna face," Vivian said. "Ben Torrey was her husband. She claimed he wrote *Tourist Trap* and Joanna stole it. She never mentioned her name?"

"Not to me she didn't. I not sure she ever knew her name. But some woman threatened her before, you know," Neville said. "Perhaps it was Sylvia Torrey."

Vivian and Freddie exchanged glances.

"No, we didn't know," Freddie said.

"She showed up at another reading."

"Where?"

"L.A. It seems she was following Joanna on her tour, stalking her, I guess you'd call it. She had a copy of the book with her and when she handed it to Joanna during the signing Joanna saw that she had written *You will pay for what you did.*"

"Sounds like a death threat," Freddie said.

"Yes, I took it that way too," Neville said. "It left Joanna shaken. I think she was beginning to regret that the book was so successful because this woman wouldn't leave her alone." Neville smiled sadly. "But she'll have to leave her alone now, won't she?"

"Did you tell the police what you've told us?" Freddie said.

"Yes, I called them when I heard what happened. But I'm afraid I wasn't much help." She gave a rueful smile. "I probably haven't been much help to you either."

Freddie smiled. "On the contrary you've been most helpful." He stood. "We won't take up any more of your time." He looked at Vivian. "Shall we go?"

NINETEEN

"Do you think they were lovers?" Vivian said as Freddie jumped on Highway 24 and drove west toward San Francisco. It was mid-afternoon and the traffic rolling toward the Caldecott Tunnel was still light. But once they cleared the tunnel and headed toward the Bay Bridge they would crawl all the way to the city.

Freddie gave her a cheeky glance. "No, but you were," he said with a teasing smile.

"C'mon, I'm being serious."

"So am I. You owe me a story, love. Remember?"

"Yeah, I remember," Vivian said. "But this is more important."

"Not to my readers it's not."

"Seriously, what do you think?"

"I think they were friends, nothing more."

"I think she believed the rumors."

"Must be tough to think the worst about a friend."

"Yes, I suppose it is," Freddie said. He chuckled. "In my line of work you think the worst about everybody."

"What do you think about the fact that Torrey was stalking her? If it was Torrey?"

"I think it makes her look like the killer. I mean, it's circumstantial evidence, but it all points in her direction."

"Why did she take the next step? I mean, what pushed her over the edge?"

Freddie shrugged. "Her husband's suicide?"

Vivian looked at him. "We should check him out."

"We?"

"Come on, Freddie, you know what I mean."

"Why?"

"I don't know, exactly." Then, as if the idea had just occurred to her, Vivian said, "What if he didn't kill himself? What if *he* was murdered?"

Freddie scoffed. Him too, huh? You've been reading too many mysteries, love."

"Just look into it, okay?" Vivian glanced at the clock on the dash. "Shit. Donny's gonna kill me."

"Donny?"

"My boss."

TWENTY

"Give me one good reason why I shouldn't fire your lululemon ass right now." Donny said. He was sitting back in his Aeron chair with his Nikes up on his desk as usual and his hands behind his head.

Vivian said nothing. She stood before him and stared at the bamboo floor. She felt as if she was trying to juggle two versions of herself, and it was getting harder and harder to pull it off.

"What the hell you think we got going on here, Vivian? You know how many copywriters would kill for your job?"

"Sorry, Donny, it won't happen again," Vivian said.

"Yeah, if I fire you it's definitely not gonna happen again. What the hell's going on with you?"

"It's personal," Vivian said. "I'd rather not talk about it."

"Look I don't care what you do on your own time, but I do care about losing clients. You feel me?"

Vivian nodded.

"I don't get it, Vivian. This isn't like you. Before you used to sit in your cubicle like a quiet little mouse and read at lunch. Now you're gone for three, four hours doing I don't know what. You're a good copywriter and I don't want to lose you, but I'm worried that maybe I already have."

"I'm sorry."

"You better be more than sorry, Vivian, or your ass is history. This is your last warning. I've cut you some slack but now you owe me. So get back to your desk and stay there. The *Cloud Cover* copy's due by the end of the day, and it better be good."

Vivian did as she was told and went back to her cubicle. Terry was waiting for her with his arms crossed, leaning against the divider that separated his cubicle from hers.

"Don't say it," Vivian said as she came up to him.

"Say what?"

"I don't know. Whatever you were gonna say."

"Well, *excuse* me," Terry said.

Vivian looked at him. "Don't go all queen on me, okay? I'm not in the mood." She brushed past Terry, sat down at her desk and awakened her computer.

"Well, you're not packing up so I guess Donny Dumb didn't fire you."

"Not yet, anyway."

"Yeah, especially if you keep playing detective."

Vivian looked sharply at Terry, her eyes flashing with anger and defiance.

"Who says I'm playing, Terry? I told you this was important to me."

"So is paying the rent."

Vivian sighed. "Yeah, I know. Speaking of which, I'm on deadline."

"Okay. Let me know if you want to do a little happy hour after work."

"Yeah, sure, I'll let you know," Vivian said.

Vivian stayed late to finish the copy for the new *Cloud Cover* ad, then emailed it to Donny and waited for his reply. She knew she couldn't leave until she'd heard back from him. Especially since she'd been gone half the day.

Donny approved the copy and told Vivian he would send it off to the client. She was done for the day. Terry reminded her of happy hour as she was preparing to leave, but that in turn just reminded Vivian of Joanna, who was happy one moment, then dead the next.

And so she took another rain check and told Terry that she needed to go home and try to put her life back together.

TWENTY-ONE

RITTER WATCHES SYLVIA AS SHE STANDS BY THE UPSTAIRS WINDOW OF HIS building and looks down at the buses in the parking lot. She's still wearing her Safeway uniform. But not for long, he thinks as he watches her. She tells him that she should lose a few pounds but Ritter tells her he likes the padding.

"Why do you live here anyway? It's like you're always at work." She says this without turning around. Then she takes a sip of the drink in her hand.

Ritter smiles. He's wearing a wife-beater and sitting in the faded and torn leather club chair he found at a garage sale in south city.

"How many buses do you have?"

"Just the two."

"You like talking about the murders, don't you?"

He sips his drink. "Is that what you're thinking about? Murder?"

Sylvia turns to face him. "I was thinking about her."

"Joanna?"

"How did you know?"

Ritter shrugs. "She was famous. It's all over the news. Everybody's talking about her."

"She was a thief," Sylvia says.

"Maybe it was just a coincidence."

Sylvia stiffens. "Like hell it was a coincidence. She stole Ben's book."

Ritter nods, then sips his drink. "By the way, now that you mention it, you never told me where Ben got the idea for his book."

Sylvia flashes a nervous smile. "Does it matter?"

Ritter shrugs. "Just curious, that's all."

"I don't know...I guess he just made it up, you know, that's what writers do." She gulps her drink.

"Yeah, I guess so," Ritter says. "Unless you're Joanna Rorke. Then you just steal it. Download it onto a flash drive and you're done, right?"

"She got what was coming to her," Sylvia says in a bitter voice.

Ritter stands and walks over to Sylvia and puts his arms around her. He can feel the tension in her body. His stubble grazes her neck.

"What about me, baby?" Ritter says as he unzips her uniform. "Am I gonna get what's coming to me?"

She looks up at him. "Why me? I'm nothing special."

"I wouldn't say that, Sylvia. I'd say you're real special."

"Yeah? Why? What's so fucking special about me, Floyd?"

"Ask Ben. He thought you were special."

Sylvia scoffs. "Yeah, right. I just wasn't special enough for him to stick around."

"I'm not going anywhere," Ritter says as he cups his hands around her breasts.

"We shouldn't do this anymore," she says firmly.

"Why? Don't you like it anymore?"

"No, it's not that."

"Then what is it?"

Sylvia pauses. "Maybe that was part of why he killed himself."

Ritter pulls back and looks at her "What are you talking about?"

"Maybe he found out about us, and between that and the book it was too much for him."

"Is that what you think?"

"I don't know. What if it's true?"

"Doesn't matter now, does it?"

"I feel guilty."

"We're all guilty, baby, one way or another," Ritter says, and when he looks down at her he can see the fear in her eyes.

TWENTY-TWO

By the time Vivian got home she felt as if she was about to crash. Moonlighting as a detective was beginning to take its toll. But as she approached her apartment she saw at once that something was wrong. The door was ajar, as if someone had forced it open. *Were they still inside?* she wondered. Vivian stood by the door as the fear that began in the pit of her stomach climbed into her throat. She looked around but saw no one.

She was alone. What was she supposed to do now? Wake a neighbor and ask them if they saw anyone? Call the police? *No, not the police,* she told herself. It would only add to their suspicions. As for the neighbors, they were probably asleep when it happened and would tell her they saw nothing. Break-ins were a common occurrence in the city. Residents shrugged, took inventory of what had been stolen, then changed the locks and went on with their lives. But getting ripped off was anything but common for Vivian, as it was the first time it had happened to her.

She cautiously pushed the door open a few inches. "Hello, anybody there?"

No answer. Vivian took a deep breath, then pushed the door open and walked into her apartment. What she saw took her breath away.

The place was a shambles. It was as if a hurricane had struck her apartment. Books had been thrown out of the bookcase and hurled across the room. The chairs and the coffee table had been upended and the Crate and Barrel sofa she bought on sale was resting on its side. The cushions were on the floor by the windows. She went into the kitchen and found her dishes in pieces on the floor. Vivian could feel herself trembling as she surveyed the damage. *Who did this?* she wondered, *and why? What were they looking for?* The rage with which everything had been torn apart terrified her. She felt as if they would have torn her apart if she had been there.

Vivian went down to Shondra's apartment, which was directly below hers, and knocked on the door. She could hear deep bass hip-hop pumping through the walls. Then Shondra opened the door. She was wearing shorts and a tank top that showed off her nipples. The pungent smell of marijuana drifted out into the corridor.

"Hey girl," she said with a smile, "What's up?"

"I got broken into," Vivian said. "Just wondered if you heard anything?"

Shondra gave a shocked look. "Bummer. When?"

"I don't know, today sometime."

"I didn't hear anything. Must've been the music."

"Who is it?" a man said from inside, in a voice that Vivian recognized immediately. Then Jake appeared in the doorway. He tensed when he saw her. "Hey..."

Vivian's face tightened. She gave Jake a withering look. "You just can't help yourself, can you, Jake?"

Shondra gave an awkward smile. "We're just hanging out..."

"Well, don't let me stop you," Vivian said. She went back up to her apartment, then pulled out her cell phone and punched in a number. "Can you come over, please?" she said, on the brink of tears.

TWENTY-THREE

FREDDIE STOOD IN THE MIDDLE OF THE ROOM WITH HIS HANDS ON HIS hips and looked around Vivian's studio apartment.

"Bloody hell, this looks worse than my place," he said.

Vivian remained by the door, as if too frightened to venture any further into her own apartment. "I'm scared. What if they come back?"

"You can't stay here tonight, love."

Vivian looked at Freddie. "Excuse me? What do you mean, I can't stay here? This is my apartment. I *live* here, okay? What am I supposed to do, go to a motel or something?"

"Come stay with me tonight."

Vivian stared at Freddie. "You?"

"Blimey, I'm not that bad, am I?"

"Why am I gonna stay with you?"

"Because you never get a wink of sleep in this mess, that's why. And you said it yourself – what if they come back?"

"I'll be fine," Vivian said. "People get robbed all the time, right?"

Freddie shrugged. "Suit yourself, then. You want me to help you sort this out a bit before I leave?"

Vivian shook her head. "It's okay, I'll deal with it."

But it wasn't okay. The break-in had left her feeling as if she had been personally invaded. She had read about people who said that getting robbed made them feel as if they'd been raped. That pretty much described the way Vivian was feeling. And it embarrassed her to have Freddie see her after she'd been violated. Even if she did call him and ask for his help. But what kind of help did she want? He had offered to put her up for the night; why did she turn him down? She had no idea. Everything was a jumble in her head, like the shambles of what once had been her home.

Freddie headed for the door.

"Thanks for coming back," Vivian said.

Freddie nodded and opened the door. Then he looked at Vivian with a puzzled expression. "Why'd you call me?"

"I was scared."

"And now?"

Vivian shrugged.

"You shouldn't be alone right now," Freddie said.

"I'm alone a lot," Vivian said with a shrug. "Why should tonight be any different?"

"Well, I'll say goodnight, then," Freddie said, and stepped out of the apartment.

Vivian remained by the door, as if unsure what to do next. But nothing was not an option. And so she slowly began putting the room back together again. She tipped the sofa back on its feet, replaced the cushions and turned the chairs and coffee table right side up. She was about to start picking up the books that were scattered on the floor when she changed her mind.

Freddie was getting into the Jag when Vivian came running out of the building. "Freddie!" she shouted. "Wait!"

Freddie looked up and saw Vivian coming toward him, a blue lululemon bag on her shoulder.

"What if it wasn't a break-in?" Vivian said as they rolled down empty streets toward Freddie's apartment in the Haight.

Freddie looked at her. "What the devil was it then? Looked like a break-in to me."

"What if it was about the case?"

"What do you mean?"

"What if they were looking for something?"

Freddie glanced at her. "What?"

"I don't know."

Freddie turned the ignition key. The starter motor cranked but the car failed to start.

"What's the matter?" Vivian said.

"Just needs a bit of coaxing from time to time," Freddie said as he continued cranking the starter.

"You're gonna run down the battery."

"Not to worry, love," he said as the engine finally fired.

"I guess it's true what they say about British cars, huh?"

Freddie's eyes narrowed as the Jag pulled away from the curb and rolled through a deserted intersection.

TWENTY-FOUR

"WELL, HERE WE ARE," FREDDIE SAID AFTER THEY HAD TRUDGED UP THE stairs to his third-floor walkup. He unlocked the door, then stepped aside. "After you."

Vivian walked past him into a stuffy, cramped one-bedroom apartment that smelled of cigarettes and appeared to be in a permanent state of disarray. Everywhere Vivian looked she saw dirty dishes, pizza boxes, takeout cartons, clothes, old magazines and newspapers, empty bottles and cans, half-filled cups and glasses, ashtrays filled to overflowing and worn furniture that was covered with fur balls and sagged under the weight of years of use.

"Don't mind the mess," Freddie said, "I don't." He chuckled at his joke.

For Vivian, a woman who liked things neat and tidy and fervently believed that less was more, the disarray was nearly suffocating. She had no idea how she was going to survive the night. Or the smell. But then she remembered why she was there.

Two cats, a tabby and a calico, were curled up on the sofa. They looked up at Freddie and Vivian.

"Hello, me lovelies," Freddie said, smiling affectionately at the cats.

The calico took one look at Vivian and jumped off the sofa and ran into another room.

"Don't mind Claire, she'll come round," Freddie said, as the tabby rubbed up against him. Freddie reached down and petted him. "Nigel, say hello to Vivian." Freddie looked at Vivian. "You like cats?"

Vivian made a face. "I'm allergic," she said, and immediately sneezed.

"Pity. They're me life," Freddie said. "Don't know where I'd be without 'em." He looked around the room. "You take the bedroom, I'll take the sofa."

"You sure? I don't mind—"

"Quite," Freddie said. "The bedroom's this way. Just need to straighten up a bit."

Vivian followed him toward the bedroom., but then stopped at the door. The bed was unmade and clothes and shoes were scattered everywhere.

"You'll have to excuse me," Freddie said, a sheepish look on his face. "I don't often have overnight guests."

"It's okay," Vivian said, but the truth was that being in Freddie's bedroom, seeing his unmade bed, was way too intimate, and she felt awkward and out of place. They were strangers thrown together by circumstance. But she could hardly blame him, seeing as how she had asked for his help. In fact, if there was anyone was to blame it was her. If she hadn't taken it upon herself to investigate Joanna's murder none of this would have happened.

"It's a bit awkward isn't it," he said.

"Yeah, I guess so. I mean, I appreciate you putting up for the night…it's just…."

"I'm not quite the man of your dreams, am I? If you're going to find yourself in a man's bedroom this isn't what you imagined, is it?"

"That's not what I meant."

"Well, it may not be what you meant, but that's what it is. Look, I'm too old to take offense, Vivian. We both know why you're here, and it's better for you that you are here, given what happened to your apartment."

"They're just trying to scare me off."

"Yes, they are. And I'd say so far they're doing a pretty good job of it."

"I'm not giving up, Freddie. You can bail if you want. But I hope you won't because I can't do this alone."

"Yes, well, let's hope it doesn't get us both killed." Freddie scanned the bedroom, then said, "I'll just tidy up a bit and then we can both get some sleep. How's that sound?"

"Sounds good, thanks."

Freddie gathered up the clothes and shoes and tossed them into the closet in no particular order. Then he looked at the bed.

"I expect you'd like clean sheets," he said.

"That would be great," Vivian said with a grateful smile.

"I'll just be a moment."

Freddie stepped out of the bedroom, then reappeared moments later with a set of clean sheets and began stripping the bed.

"You want some help?" Vivian said.

Freddie shook his head. "I've got it. Won't take a moment."

Freddie made the bed, then stepped back and admired his handiwork. "There, that's better," he said. He looked at Vivian. "All yours, love. Sleep tight." Then he bundled up the dirty sheets and pillowcases and walked out of the bedroom and closed the door behind him.

Vivian looked around the room, then sat on the bed, which, surprisingly, was more comfortable than she had expected it to be. She felt homeless, even though she knew she wasn't. But she had been driven from her home by a threat that, as Freddie warned, would only get worse. *What am I doing, playing girl detective? What I have to,* she told herself. But she wondered if she was getting in too deep to ever get out again. Right now, however, she was dead on her feet and had no idea how she was going to get up in time for a 9am staff meeting.

Vivian took off her clothes, then pulled a pair of pajamas out of her overnight bag and put them on. She turned off the light and climbed into Freddie's bed. In the dark she could hear Freddie talking to Nigel and Claire in that soft, gentle voice that people used when they talked to their pets. So different from what she heard when she crawled into bed at home. Then it was clang of the cable cars, which ran until midnight. Or the sounds of her neighbors' lives, which bled through the walls. But she was far from home tonight, and her journey had only just begun.

Vivian woke in the dark from a dream she could not remember. She no idea what time it was or, for a moment, where she was. Then, as her eyes became accustomed to the dark, it came to her that she was alone in another man's bed for reasons that had nothing to do with sex or love or romance. All the things that an unmarried woman her age was supposed to care about. Indeed, the only reason she was in Freddie's bed was murder. She glanced at the clock on the nightstand, then got up to use the toilet. As she made her way to the bathroom she peeked into the living room. Freddie sat at his desk. He was hunched over his laptop, smoking a cigarette and wearing a rumpled bathrobe. Claire was curled up in his lap and Nigel was spread out on the desk. A lamp illuminated Freddie and his cats while leaving the rest of the room in shadows.

"What are you doing? It's three in the morning," Vivian said.

Freddie looked up at her. "Sorry, love, I didn't wake you did I?"

"No, but what are you doing?"

"Reading a coroner's report. Ben Torrey. Fascinating reading in the middle of the night."

"Sylvia's husband?" Vivian said with interest as she walked over to him.

"The coroner ruled it a suicide," Freddie said.

"How'd he do it?"

"You want the gory details, do you?"

"Yeah, I do," Vivian said, then sneezed.

"Bless you," Freddie said.

"Do you mind?" Vivian said, nodding at the cigarette.

"Sorry, love," Freddie said, and stubbed out the cigarette in an ashtray overflowing with butts. "He gassed himself in his car. A vintage BMW, actually. Terrible thing to do a car like that, fill it with carbon monoxide."

"So that's that, then. Sylvia was telling the truth."

Freddie scrunched up his face. "Not quite," he said.

"What do you mean?"

"They found drugs in his system, tranquilizers."

"You think he was trying to calm down before he did it?"

"Maybe. Or maybe somebody helped him."

Vivian stared at Freddie. "Helped him how?"

"Well, the trouble is there's no way of knowing whether he took the drugs voluntarily, or whether they were forcibly administered."

"Which would make it murder."

"Possibly. But if it was murder made up to look like suicide, who did it and why?"

"Sylvia said he killed himself because Joanna stole his book."

"Yes, and perhaps he did. But was that enough reason for the man to commit suicide? A bit extreme, if you ask me. Mind you, I'm not saying it was murder…I'm just saying that in a case like this it seems as if it could have gone either way."

Freddie and Vivian fell silent. Claire picked up her head and looked at Vivian, then went back to sleep. Nigel, on the other hand, slept through the whole thing.

"What made you think of him?"

Freddie shrugged. "I couldn't sleep, and for some reason it put me in mind of Ben Torrey, so I decided to take a look at the coroner's report. Thought I'd poke around a bit and see what I could find."

"That reminds me," Vivian said, "there's something I want to take a look at."

"What?"

"I'll be right back." Vivian went back into the bedroom, then emerged moments later with a flash drive.

"What's this?" Freddie said.

"Sylvia Torrey gave it to me. She said the manuscript for *Tourist Trap* was on it. She wanted me to read it so I could see how it was the same as Joanna's book, *The Murder Tour*."

"Let's have a look then, shall we?" Freddie said.

He inserted the flash drive into his laptop. A moment later, the icon appeared on the desktop. Freddie clicked on it and the title page of a manuscript appeared on the screen. But instead of *Tourist Trap* it read: *Death Trip by Floyd Ritter*. There was a handwritten note on the title page that read *We did it, baby. The book is all yours.*

Vivian and Freddie exchanged glances.

"What's *Death Trip?*" Freddie said.

"Who's Floyd Ritter?" Vivian said.

"Yes, and what the devil does the note mean, *We did it.*'" Freddie looked up at Vivian. "Who did what?"

TWENTY-FIVE

RITTER OPENS THE DOOR AND CARRIES A PORTABLE VACUUM, BROOM, dustpan, paper towels and cleaning supplies onto the bus. It's early and he has to clean the bus before the first tour of the day. He has to clean it after every tour because people are filthy and spread their dirt wherever they go. Especially tourists, who seem to think that they have a right to soil whatever they touch. If the bus was a public toilet they'd never flush after using it.

People often ask him why he doesn't hire a cleaning service to maintain the bus. Ritter tells them that cleaning services are too expensive and don't do a good job. After all, who wants to clean a bus for a living? But the real reason is that they ask too many questions about the tour. Questions about the murders. Ritter doesn't like to talk about the tour for free. The way he feels about it, if they want to know what he knows about the murders, they should buy a ticket. Then he'll tell them all about it.

Ritter scowls as he stands in the aisle and looks around. Tourist trash is everywhere. Crumpled soda cans, coffee cups, fast-food wrappers, half-eaten candy bars – the bus is littered with garbage. There's a sign posted by the door that says no eating or drinking, but no one pays any attention to it. And he's too busy driving the bus and entertaining the passengers to monitor whether anyone is violating his rules. But the truth is, they all are. And he knows that if he threw everyone he caught eating or drinking off the bus, word would get around and he'd go out of business.

So he puts up with it. Just as he puts up with everything else. He pulls on his gloves and sweeps the cans, wrappers and other trash into the dustpan and dumps it all into a black plastic garbage bag. As he does so, he flashes on how he wishes he could sweep up the passengers and dump *them* into a garbage bag. The thought brings a grim smile to his face. He switches on the vacuum and runs it over and under the seats, then uses Windex and paper towels to clean all the windows, which are dirty and greasy from tourists pressing their faces against the glass. As if that would bring them closer to what it's like to take a life.

It's their fault he has to do this, work as a janitor and a bus driver just to make a living. If it wasn't for them he would free and clear of it all now, free of the tourists and the need to clean up after them. Someone else would have to drive the bus then, but it wouldn't be Floyd Ritter. Not by a long shot. He's learned what he needs to learn driving the bus, and now it's time to step off. But instead they stole his future.

He finishes cleaning the bus, picks up the broom and vacuum and carries them across the lot to his office. He sets them by the door, as he does every day, then heads back to the bus for the rest of his cleaning supplies. But just then the sun rises over the south of Market rooftops, and as he looks at the bus glowing in the morning light, Ritter imagines setting it on fire with everyone onboard.

Famous murders are way more fun than ordinary murders, and Murder Tours has them all.

RALPH AND HELEN PERLMUTTER, DES MOINES, IA

TWENTY-SIX

VIVIAN GLANCED AT THE CLOCK ON FREDDIE'S NIGHTSTAND AS SHE stuffed her things into her overnight bag. It was 8am and she had an hour to get to work in time for a staff meeting. Showing up late to a Donny Dumbarton meeting amounted to a capital offense, as they were command performances for a captive audience.

She zipped up the bag and walked into the kitchen. Saw Freddie feeding Nigel and Claire, and sneezed.

Freddie gave her an apologetic look. "Sorry, love," he said.

"It's okay. You gonna drop me off or should I get an Uber or something?" Vivian asked.

Freddie petted Nigel and Claire as they ate.

"Not to worry, love, I'll drop you."

"Okay then, we gotta go, like now," Vivian said.

"Right you are," Freddie said. "I'll just get me coat and me keys." He pulled on a jacket, then looked around the room. "Now where the devil did I leave them?"

Vivian's face creased with impatience. "You're kidding me. You lost your keys?"

"Ah, here they are," Freddie said, retrieving his keys from under an old magazine. He looked at Vivian. "Shall we?"

Just then there was a knock at the door.

Freddie glanced at his watch. "Bit early for visitors," he said to himself as he stepped across the room.

He opened it to see a leggy redhead in her late 40s or early 50s standing there.

"Hello, Freddie," she said in a Cockney accent, "remember me?"

A broad smile spread across Freddie's face. "Hello, Barbara," he said, and gave her a hug. "What are you doing here?"

"I've got a layover between flights and thought I'd look you up." Barbara walked into the apartment. "Happy to see me?"

"Very happy to see you," Freddie said. "It's been awhile."

"Ten years," Barbara said. She glanced at Vivian. "A bit young for you, isn't she, Freddie?" she said with a knowing smile.

Freddie grinned. "This is Vivian. We work together. Vivian, say hello to Barbara."

"Hi," Vivian said, confused by the sudden turn of events.

"Me and Freddie go way back, don't we, love?"

"That we do," Freddie said. "Barbara was my steady back in the day. So how you getting on? Still a flight attendant?"

"Flying international for British Airways. Heading back to London day after tomorrow."

"Sounds a bit posh," Freddie said.

"More like being a waitress," Barbara said, a wry look on her face.

"Fancy a cup of tea? I'll put the kettle on."

"I'd love it."

Vivian's face creased with concern. "Freddie, I gotta get to work, remember?"

"Oh right..." Freddie said, as if he'd just remembered that he'd offered to drive Vivian to the agency.

"You have to go out?" Barbara said. "Am I being a bother?"

"I'll get a cab or an Uber," Vivian said, "don't worry about it."

"You sure?" Freddie said.

"Yeah, no problem."

"So I'll see you later?" Barbara said. She nodded at Freddie. "We have to catch up about Freddie."

"Sure," Vivian said, deciding that she liked her.

Donny's weekly staff meeting was the last thing on Vivian's mind as she walked into reception. She had spent half the night reading over Freddie's shoulder as he scrolled through the pages of the manuscript they found on the flash drive. As she did so it soon became clear that *Death Trip* and *The Murder Tour* told the same story —a serial killer murdering tourists who went on murder tours in San Francisco. According to Sylvia Torrey, that was also the plot of *Tourist Trap*. But which came first? Who stole from whom? And why did Sylvia give her *Death Trip* instead of *Tourist Trap*? And who was Floyd Ritter? And what was the meaning of the note scrawled on the title page? Vivian had no idea.

But as she walked into the conference room, she was feeling strung out from lack of sleep and sure that it showed. She was also wearing the same clothes she wore to work the day before. She was sure that showed as well. The meeting was already underway but Donny raised his hand to halt the proceedings when Vivian made her entrance.

"Hey, look who's here," Donny said. "Glad you could make it, Vivian. It's just not the same without you." He looked around the conference table. "Is it, team?"

"No!" everyone said in unison, their voices crashing over Vivian like a wave.

"Hot date last night?" Donny said.

Titters surfaced from one end of the table to the other. Vivian forced a smile and thought about whether anyone would notice if she crawled under the table. Instead, she pulled out a chair and sat down next to Terry, who gave her one of his *What's up with you?* looks.

"My apartment got broken into," Vivian said. "That's why I'm late."

Donny faked a sympathetic face and said, "Oh no, sorry, to hear it, Vivian," as the staff followed up with a chorus of *Aw, geez, bummer, that really sucks,* etc.

"Sorry, girlfriend," Terry said, giving Vivian a hug. "What'd they take?"

"I don't know yet," Vivian said, "the place is a mess."

"I think you could use a hug, Viv," Donny said. "What do you think, team? Shall we give her a hug?"

"Yes!"

"That's okay," Vivian said, dreading the group hug.

But to no avail. She was forced to stand up as a line formed and everyone took a turn and gave her a hug.

"Feel better now?" Donny said.

Vivian forced a polite smile and sat down.

"Okay, let's get back to work," Donny said. "Where were we?"

"You were telling us about your super lunch with the *Cloud Cover* client," Kelli Cleavage said in her best suck-up voice.

"Oh right." He looked at Vivian. "Which reminds me. How we doing on the tagline, Vivian?"

"I came up with a new one."

"We're all ears," Donny said.

"A Better Cloud for Better Business," Vivian said.

Donny stared at the ceiling as he considered it, then let a satisfied smile spread across his face.

"I like it."

"Thanks."

"Let's run it by the client and see if he likes it too."

The meeting droned on, but as the spotlight shifted to other staff members, Vivian tuned out. She had other things on her mind, like the discovery of *Death Trip*, an author named Floyd Ritter and an apartment in shambles. And the more she thought about it, the more she became convinced that they were all connected. Whoever tore her place apart was looking for something. But what? And what would they do next? Come after her again? She shivered as the fear ran down her spine. Terry looked at her.

"You cold?"

"It's just the AC," Vivian said, "it always gives me chills."

"This wouldn't have anything to do with you playing girl detective, would it?" Terry said as they walked back to their cubicles after the meeting.

Vivian said nothing.

"I knew it!" Terry said. "You're getting yourself in way deep, aren't you?"

"I need to know why she was killed."

"Why? So you can be next?"

TWENTY-SEVEN

A PLAYER WEARING A RED AND YELLOW JERSEY AND SHORTS PROPELLED A ball across a vibrantly green field and scored a goal as the crowd roared. Barbara looked up at the flat-screen TV mounted on the wall above the bar.

"Arsenal versus Manchester United," she said. She looked at Freddie. "Like old times, eh?" she said.

Freddie nodded. "Quite."

"How long ago, Freddie?"

Freddie gave a shrug. "I haven't seen you in years."

"Has it been that long?"

Freddie looked fondly at Barbara. "Too long, love."

A barmaid came up to the table. They were at *The Pig and Whistle*, a crowded English pub on Geary Boulevard in the Laurel District. Men and women with beer mugs in their hands were playing darts, watching the game and shouting orders at the bartender.

"What's it gonna be then?" the barmaid said in a south London accent.

"Bangers and mash for me, love," Freddie said. "And a Newcastle Brown Ale." He looked at Barbara.

"The same for me," Barbara said.

"Easy, then," the barmaid said with a smile.

"So when's your flight?" Freddie said after the barmaid had moved away from the table.

"Day after tomorrow."

"Doesn't give us much time, does it?"

"More time than we've had in years," Barbara said.

"You should've come with me, love," Freddie said.

Barbara sighed. "Oh Freddie, we went over all that years ago. Maybe you should've stayed."

The barmaid returned with two pints of Newcastle Brown Ale. Freddie picked up his mug.

"Here's to us…now and then," he said.

"How about just now?" Barbara said. "It's all we've got left, love."

Freddie gave a rueful nod. "I'll drink to that," he said. He leaned in and kissed Barbara on the cheek. She gave Freddie a tender smile and they both took sips of their ale.

"So tell me, Freddie, what are you up to with Vivian? You're a bit of an odd couple, you know."

Freddie chuckled. "Yes, I suppose we are, but it's nothing like that, love. I'm working on a case with her."

"You mean a story?"

"Well, I suppose it's both a story and a case."

"You playing detective now, are you? Shouldn't you leave that to the coppers?"

"Yes, I should, love. But it's a good story, and if I can crack the case I'll keep my job."

"What do you mean, you'll keep your job?"

"I haven't broken a story in a long time and they're just waiting for an excuse to push me out, along with all the other older reporters. They want to make room for the young ones and all they need is an excuse."

"But you've got the experience…all those years on Fleet Street…"

Freddie scoffed. "They don't care about experience. They think they can get it on the cheap. The world belongs to the young, in case you hadn't noticed."

"I try not to," Barbara said, and took a sip of her ale. "So tell me about the case...or the story, or whatever it is you're working on with Vivian."

The barmaid returned with their orders of bangers and mash.

"Lovely," Barbara said, looking down at the plate. "Just like the place we used to go to in Windsor Street. What was it called?"

"The Black Horse."

"Ah yes, the Black Horse. Those were the days, eh?"

Freddie nodded, his mind flooded with memories of London afternoons with Barbara years ago.

"So... about the case," Barbara said, digging into her bangers and mash.

While they ate, Freddie braced Barbara on what he knew about the Joanna Rorke case. When he was finished, Barbara just stared at him for a few moments, as if she needed the time to absorb what Freddie had told her.

"She spent the night with her?" Barbara said.

Freddie nodded.

"And then found her dead in the morning?"

"Murdered."

"Blimey, that's a hell of a story."

"Yes, it is."

But what about the coppers?"

"What about them?"

"Aren't they investigating?"

"Yes, I suppose they are."

"What if they find out what you're up to?"

Freddie shrugged. "They won't like it, I reckon."

"No, they won't, and then what? Is it worth the risk?"

Freddie paused to think about it. He gazed into his mug, as if it held the answer. Then he looked up at Barbara and, with a sardonic smile, said, "I hope so."

TWENTY-EIGHT

THE DOOR WAS OPEN.

The lights were on.

Vivian could hear someone moving around inside her apartment.

What sounded like the *thwack* of books hitting the wall. She stopped cold as fear took hold of her. Had the thief returned to search for what he missed the first time around? Or was he back for her? How did she know it was a him? She had no idea who it was. Only that they were in her home. She fought an impulse to run out of the building and slowly approached the door. She cautiously pushed it open, then rolled her eyes.

"What are you doing here, Hannah?"

Hannah, who was in the process of putting books back in the bookcase, looked over at her sister. Vivian could tell that she had already put the furniture back in place and generally straightened out the apartment, which no longer looked as if a hurricane had blown in through the window. She saw a bottle of Chardonnay and a wine glass on the coffee table and wondered how long Hanna had been there.

"What's it look like I'm doing, Viv?" Hannah said. "What the fuck happened here?"

"Somebody broke in."

"Bastards. What'd they take?"

"Nothing."

Hannah looked at her. "Excuse me? They broke in but they didn't take anything?"

Vivian nodded. "I guess I didn't have anything they wanted."

Hannah put the stack of books in her arms in the bookcase, then flopped on the sofa. She picked up the glass of Chardonnay and took a sip.

"What's going on, little sis? I get the feeling there's something you're not telling me."

"What are you doing here, anyway?"

"I was in town and thought I'd see if you wanted to grab a bite."

"Where are the boys?"

"Dan took them bowling. I told him I wanted to go shopping and get my hair done." She took another sip of Chardonnay. "That's my story. What's yours?"

Vivian sighed. She went into the kitchen for another wine glass, then poured herself some wine. She took a sip, then looked at her sister.

"It's about the murder."

"The writer who was killed, the one you spent the night with?"

Vivian nodded.

"What's that got to do with you? It's over, isn't it? Aren't the police investigating?"

"I guess they are, but it's not over, not for me anyway."

"What are you talking about?"

"Whoever broke in was looking for something in particular."

"What?"

"I don't know."

"You're losing me, Viv."

Vivian paused. This was the hard part. "I'm on the case, Hannah. Me and this crime reporter from *The San Francisco Sentinel*."

Hannah stared at her sister. "You're kidding me, right?"

But the look on Vivian's face told Hannah she was dead serious.

"What do you mean, you're on the case? You're not a cop, you're a copywriter, for God's sake."

"I need to know what happened."

"So wait for the cops to figure out what happened. Why do you have to get involved?"

Vivian glanced at all the mysteries in her bookcase. Hannah followed her line of sight.

"They're just books, Viv, they're not real life."

"This is my chance, Hannah. Don't you see?"

"I'll tell you what I see, sis. I see this as your chance to get thrown in jail or worse. Don't you see that?"

'Remember when we were kids, Hannah? Every time I wanted to do something you were there to tell me I shouldn't do it because I was only asking for trouble. You remember that?"

"Yeah, I remember. I remember I was right most of the time. And this time you're definitely asking for trouble."

"You made me afraid to do what I wanted to do. But I'm not afraid anymore. I mean, I am, but I'm not gonna let it stop me. Not this time."

"Okay, I guess we're done here then," Hannah said. She drained her glass and stood.

Vivian looked up at her. "Don't be mad, Hannah."

"I'm not mad, Viv, I'm just really, really worried, okay?"

Vivian stood and embraced her sister. "Thanks for putting the place back together."

Hannah gave a wry smile. "I hope we don't have to put you back together. I don't suppose I could talk you into staying with us until all this blows over."

Vivian smiled and shook her head.

"Didn't think so."

Vivian walked Hannah to the door and they embraced again.

"Be careful," Hannah said. "I don't want to lose the only sister I've got."

"I promise," Vivian said.

Then Hannah was gone and Vivian was left alone with her thoughts. She refilled her glass, then surveyed her apartment which, thanks to Hannah, was back to normal. But it was an illusion, because nothing in Vivian's life was normal now.

TWENTY-NINE

THE KNOCK AT THE DOOR CAME TWO HOURS LATER. VIVIAN OPENED IT to find Detectives Bassett and Chen standing there. Their faces were set and they didn't look happy.

"Hi…" Vivian said, surprised to see them.

Bassett stepped forward and took Vivian by the shoulder, then spun her around and slapped a pair of cuffs on her.

"Hey, wait a minute, what's going on?" Vivian said, feeling the panic well up inside.

"Vivian Voss, you're under arrest for interfering with police business," Chen said. "You have the right to remain silent. Anything you say can and will be used against you in a court of law. You have the right to speak to an attorney, and to have an attorney present during questioning. If you cannot afford an attorney, one will be appointed for you. Do you understand?"

"What? What are you talking about?" Vivian said in a daze. She could feel the cuffs squeezing her wrists.

"Do you understand?" Bassett said.

Vivian nodded.

"I need to hear it," Bassett said.

"Yes, okay?" Vivian said.

They led her out of the apartment. She felt like a common criminal as they escorted her to the police car parked in front of her building and put her in the back seat.

"Am I going to jail?" Vivian said as they pulled away.

Bassett and Chen exchanged glances, but said nothing. Vivian stared through the wire mesh that separated them.

"Can't you tell me? Or isn't that allowed?'

Chen, who was driving, glanced in the rearview.

"You'll be booked and fingerprinted, that's all we can tell you at this time," he said.

"I didn't do anything," Vivian said, tears coming.

"That's not what we heard," Bassett said.

"What do you mean? What'd you hear? What did I do?"

They rolled on in silence. When they reached the police station, Vivian was booked and fingerprinted, then led into a holding cell. As the cell door slammed shut, Vivian fought to tamp down the panic that was overwhelming her. *I'm in jail,* she thought. *What if I never get out? I'll lose my job, my apartment, everything.* She sat on the bunk and buried her face in her hands.

As hour later, Bassett led her into an interrogation room. It could have been the same room she was in before; she assumed they were all the same. But she wasn't under arrest then. And she wasn't wearing handcuffs. Bassett sat down across from her. Moments later, Chen entered.

"Interfering with police is a felony, Ms. Voss," Bassett said. "It can send you to prison. Are you aware of that?"

"How was I interfering? What'd I do?'

"Your sister called us," Chen said.

Vivian swiveled to face Chen, her eyes flashing, the anger erupting inside. "Hannah? She put you up to this?"

"She told us what happened at your apartment, told us you were playing detective on the Rorke case."

"Bitch!" Vivian exploded.

"She's worried about you, Vivian."

"It was none of her business."

"Maybe not, but it's our business," Bassett said.

Vivian looked up at her, then looked away.

"We got enough to do investigating this case without you getting in the way."

"Or worse," Chen said. "Whoever murdered Joanna Rorke has already killed once, and probably won't hesitate to do it again."

"So, unless you want to find yourself facing serious jail time or lying on a slab at the morgue, leave the police work to the professionals," Bassett said.

"You've been booked on charges and fingerprinted," Chen said. "If we have to pick you up again, trust me, the DA will prosecute you. And you will go to prison. You understand?"

"Yeah, I understand," Vivian said.

"I hope so," Bassett said. "'cause it won't be pretty from here on out."

Then they took her back to her cell and gave Vivian the rest of the night to think about it.

THIRTY

THEY RELEASED VIVIAN THE NEXT DAY, JUST IN TIME FOR LUNCH. AS SHE walked out of the police station, strung out from lack of sleep and furious with her sister, Hannah, Vivian saw Freddie and Barbara in the Jaguar, which was parked at the curb. She had called Freddie when she knew she was being released. She climbed into the back seat and slammed the door.

"That good, huh?" Freddie said.

Vivian glared at him. "My fucking sister ratted me out."

"Say what?" Freddie said as he pulled away.

"The bitch turned me in. They fingerprinted me and everything. Said they'd bring me up on charges if I didn't stay out of the case."

"I was afraid something like this might happen."

"It wouldn't have happened if she'd kept her nose out of it."

Barbara, who was sitting in the front seat, swiveled and looked at Vivian. "How awful for you. Did they put the cuffs on you?"

"Manacles," Vivian said, deadpan. "They had me in chains."

Barbara turned to Freddie. "You ever go to jail, Freddie?"

"Not yet, but I expect I may soon." He glanced at Vivian in the rearview and their eyes met. "Where to, love?"

"Work. I gotta see if I still have a job."

Kelli looked up at Vivian as she walked into reception. "Donny's waiting for you in his office," she said, dispensing with any of the usual pleasantries.

"You're fired," Donny said as soon as he saw her.

Vivian froze in the doorway to his office. She could feel the panic welling up inside. She looked at Donny in dismay. "What?"

"You heard me. Clean out your desk and get out of here. And take all your damn books with you. You're done."

"Wait, Donny, I need this job…"

"Yeah, and I need somebody who's actually gonna *do* the job. Not somebody who's gonna drop in whenever she feels like it."

"Please, Donny, I'll do better, I promise."

Donny shook his head. "Do better somewhere else. You're done here."

"Donny Dumb's a jerk," Terry said as he accompanied Vivian out of the building.

"What am I gonna do now?" Vivian said.

"Get a better job," Terry said. "I'll make some calls. In the meantime, let's go have a drink and celebrate."

Vivian looked at him. "Celebrate? Hello? I just got fired."

"Look at the bright side. You'll get something better and you won't have to put up with Donny Dumb."

Vivian was not persuaded. She'd never been fired from a job before, and the shock of it was devastating. She felt as if she'd been branded as an undesirable, and the thought of going on interviews and being forced to explain why she'd been let go filled her with dread.

"I think I'm just gonna go home," she said. "I don't much feel like celebrating right now."

Terry gave a hug. "Maybe later."

"Yeah, sure, maybe later," Vivian said. But she knew that she wouldn't feel any better later than she did right now.

What she didn't count on was that she would feel even worse. Because as Vivian stepped off the cable car, she saw Hannah standing by the entrance to her building. Her face hardened. The anger she felt at seeing the person she held responsible for her overnight imprisonment raced through her like a flame.

"What the fuck are you doing here?" Vivian said.

"I called…they told me they'd released you."

"You got a lot of fucking nerve, Hannah. I just lost my job because of you. You happy now?"

"I'm so sorry, Viv, I didn't think they'd arrest you…I was just worried…"

"You were worried, huh? That's great, Hannah. Just great. You know what? I'm worried too now. I'm worried about how I'm gonna pay the rent, thanks to you."

"I just didn't want anything to happen to you. I thought—"

"I don't want to hear it, Hannah, okay? I just spent a night in jail and got fired because of you. So just go away. I got nothing to say to you."

"Vivian, please…you're my sister…"

"Not anymore," Vivian said, her eyes filling with tears. She elbowed past Hannah and went into the building.

Vivian's tears were streaming down her cheeks when she walked into her apartment. She could taste the salt on her lips, bitter as the resentment she felt toward her sister. She set the box full of her office stuff on the table, then sat on the sofa and buried her face in her hands. She and Hannah had had their share of quarrels over the years, as any two sisters would. But they were still friends, still family. The only real family that Vivian had. They had never betrayed each other, and yet now Vivian felt as if Hannah had stabbed her in the back, all in the name of protecting her from herself.

Then her phone rang. Vivian glanced at the screen. "Unknown." She took the call anyway.

"Hello?"

"I know you were there," a man said in a menacing voice. "Forget what you saw before the same thing happens to you."

Vivian heard a click as the line went dead. She felt a chill rush down her spine, as if the Angel of Death had arrived to escort her into the afterlife. She thought of her grandmother sleeping underground on a satin pillow.

He knows who I am, Vivian thought. *But how did he find me? How did he get my number?* Then she remembered jotting it down on a notepad in Joanna's room just before she left. Just before Joanna was murdered.

He must have found it, she thought, and now he's found me.

THIRTY-ONE

RITTER PICKS HER UP AFTER SHE GETS OFF AT SAFEWAY AND TAKES HER to a bar in the Mission. He's still wearing his *Murder Tours* uniform. She orders a vodka tonic and he tells the barmaid he wants a scotch rocks. When the drinks arrive they clink glasses and smile at each other. There's a football game on TV but nobody seems to be watching it. He wonders what she's thinking.

"You okay?" Ritter says. "You seem rattled."

Sylvia shrugs it off. "It's been a long day."

Ritter sips his drink.

"You happy she's dead?" he says.

"Joanna?"

"Who else?"

"She had it coming, so yeah, but it doesn't make me happy. It's just harder to keep hating her now that she's dead."

Ritter smiles and knocks back the rest of his drink.

"That's what you wanted, isn't it?"

"I did want her dead. It's her fault Ben's dead. But the trouble is she didn't just die; she was murdered. Which means that while Joanna's life has ended the case has just begun. It would've been easier if she'd been hit by a car or something." She sips her drink. "Why do you keep bringing her up all the time anyway?"

Ritter shrugs his shoulders. "I can tell it's on your mind."

"Yeah, because you won't stop talking about it."

Ritter smiles. He points at her glass. "Ready for another?"

"Sure," she says.

"One more round and then we'll go back to my place," Ritter says. "You do want that, don't you?"

"I don't know…you want it to be the way it was before."

"Don't you?"

She looks up at Ritter, and their eyes meet. But then she quickly turns away.

"Nothing's like it was before," she says. "Don't you get that?"

"You're not trying to dump me, are you, Sylvia? I think you're too scared to do that."

THIRTY-TWO

VIVIAN ROCKED BACK AND FORTH ON THE SOFA LIKE A CHILD WHO HAD no one to comfort her. Why did you have to go to her reading, why did you have to sleep with her, why did you have to give her your number? Why, why, why. The questions kept echoing over and over, louder and louder, until she thought her head would explode. *Take it easy,* she told herself. *Calm down. He doesn't know where you live. All he has is a number. Yes, but it's my number.*

She knew she should call Bassett and Chen and tell them what happened. She should have done that immediately after the call. But she needed something else now, something that the police could not provide. Then she thought of Hannah. She stood, grabbed her purse and went out the door. When she got outside she looked down the street and saw Hannah a block away. She was climbing into her SUV.

"Hannah!" Vivian shouted. "Hannah!"

Hannah looked up and saw her. She closed the car door and stepped to the sidewalk as Vivian ran down the street and into her arms.

"I'm sorry I said you weren't my sister," Vivian said. "You'll always be my sister."

Hannah smiled through the tears in her eyes. "I know. You can't get rid of me that easily. But I'm the one who should be sorry, Viv. I barged into your life and screwed everything up. This is all my fault."

"I'm scared, Hannah, and I don't know what to do."

"What happened?"

Vivian wiped her eyes and looked at her sister. "I have to talk to you. Can we go get some coffee or something?"

"Sure. I don't have to pick up the kids until three."

They went to Toast Eatery, a bacon and eggs diner on the corner of Polk and Sacramento, and grabbed a booth by the window.

Hannah reached across the table and took Vivian's hands in her own. "I'm so sorry about the job and the cops, Vivian. I just wasn't thinking, I'm such an idiot—"

"It's okay, I understand," Vivian said. "You were just trying to help." The job was the last thing on her mind.

"But I didn't help, I made everything worse."

"Everything's already worse."

"What are you saying?"

"He called me, Hannah."

"Who called you?"

"The killer. It had to be him."

Hannah took a sharp intake of breath. Her eyes widened. The color drained out of her face. She stared at her sister. "What are you talking about?"

While Hannah sipped her coffee, Vivian explained that she had jotted down her number on a notepad in Joanna's room and the killer must have seen it.

"He knows I was there," Vivian said.

"You have to tell the police. They can protect you."

Vivian scoffed. "Yeah, maybe they can lock me again."

"Maybe they should, if it'll keep you safe."

"I just feel so stupid," Vivian said. "Why did I do it?"

"You mean why did you sleep with her?"

Vivian looked into her coffee, as if it held the answer to Hannah's question.

"You wanted to," Hannah said. "You always did what you wanted.

Me, I was always afraid to do what I wanted. So I ended up with kids, a husband, a house in the suburbs and a dog." She gave a rueful smile. "I was the good girl."

"You weren't so good," Vivian said.

"Yeah, I was, compared to you. I always envied that about you, the way you could be free to do whatever you want, no matter what anybody said."

Vivian looked up at her. "Yeah, look where it got me."

"You need money for the rent?"

Vivian shook her head. "I can't take your money, Hannah."

"Sure you can. I'd take yours if I had to." Hannah paused. "Come stay with us until this all blows over."

"I can't, sis."

"Why not? Because you can't let go of it?"

Vivian shrugged. "Maybe because it can't let go of me."

Hannah's face tightened with worry. "So what are you gonna do, just wait for him to come get you?"

Vivian's cell phone rang.

"Hey, maybe it's him," she said.

She pulled the phone out of her pocket and looked at the screen and saw it was Laura Neville.

"Hi, Laura," Vivian said, surprised to hear from her.

"I hope you don't mind me calling…"

"No, of course not. What's up?"

"I didn't want to speak ill of her…"

"Joanna?"

"There's something you need to know."

THIRTY-THREE

"WHERE WERE YOU WHEN I CALLED?" VIVIAN SAID AFTER THEY'D cleared the Caldecott Tunnel.

They were in Freddie's Jaguar, heading out to Walnut Creek on Highway 24.

Freddie chuckled. "We were on a cable car. Barbara wanted to go to Fisherman's Wharf."

"What'd you tell her?"

"The truth. I had to go to work."

"You like her, don't you?"

Freddie smiled. "Yes, quite. Always have."

"How come you're not together anymore?"

Freddie glanced at Vivian and shook his head. "Not now, love, it'll just make me lonely." He paused. "Tell me about the call."

"I left my number in Joanna's room before I left. He must've found it and now he knows who I am."

"What did he say?"

"I told you what he said."

"Tell me again."

"He said I should forget what I saw unless I want to end up like her."

"Did you call the police?"

Vivian scoffed. "What are they gonna do?"

"Keep you alive."

They went up to the front door and Freddie rang the bell. A moment later Neville opened the door. She smiled politely at the sight of Vivian and Freddie on her doorstep, then looked around to see if any of her neighbors were within earshot.

"Please come in," she said, and stepped back from the door.

"I don't quite know where to begin," Neville said after she closed the door.

"You said there was something we needed to know," Vivian said.

Neville smiled politely. "Yes, there is. Please, sit down."

Freddie and Vivian sat down on the sofa. Neville perched on the edge of a chair across from them. The décor was still the same, but Vivian noticed some Nordstrom shopping bags by the door and figured Neville had been to the mall. A book of matches embossed with the name *El Rio* rested on a side table next to Neville. Vivian knew it was a dive bar in the Mission, but Neville didn't seem like the type.

Neville paused, then said, "Well, this is rather embarrassing. I guess I was still trying to protect Joanna, even though she was dead." She smiled sadly. "But I can't protect her, can I? Not anymore."

"Joanna liked to play, I suppose that would be the best way to put it."

"How do you mean?" Vivian said.

"She liked to have flings..."

"Flings?" Freddie said, jotting down some notes in his notepad.

"One-night stands, I guess you'd call them. And it didn't much matter if you were a man or a woman. All that mattered was that she wanted to play."

Vivian felt her face get hot. I was one of those flings, she thought, and look what happened.

"Unfortunately, she wasn't always careful about who she picked up."

"What happened?"

"She got in trouble with a girl she picked up who turned out to be underage."

"Jailbait," Freddie said. "I think that's what you Yanks call it."

Neville's face flushed. "Yes, I suppose that's what it was. But then the girl wanted money to keep her mouth shut."

"Who was the girl?"

"I don't remember exactly, just someone she met in a bookstore. They had a fling and then the girl threatened to go to the police if Joanna didn't pay up."

"You think she was set up?" Freddie said.

Neville shrugged. "Maybe." She chuckled to herself. "Not that Joanna needed much encouragement. She'd dive right in and to hell with the consequences."

"Where do you come in?" Vivian said.

"I was the go-between. I helped her come up with the money. Her books weren't doing so well at the time and she needed cash."

"How much cash?" Freddie said.

"The girl wanted 50 thousand."

Freddie whistled. "An expensive one-night stand."

"Yes, it was. Joanna said she'd pay me back but she never did." Neville smiled sadly. "I don't regret it. The story would've ruined her, and I never wanted that to happen."

"You ever hear from the girl again?" Freddie said.

Neville shook her head. "She got what she wanted and disappeared."

"Did it ever happen again?" Vivian said.

"No, but some people took those flings seriously. She never did. She'd just move on to the next one."

"You said some people took them seriously," Freddie said. "How seriously?"

"Well, there were hurt feelings, not that she cared about that."

"Hurt enough to want to kill her?" Vivian said.

Neville looked at her. "I wondered about that myself. There was one fellow in particular who took it hard when she dumped him. He became obsessed with her, stalking her at readings, demanding to see her, that sort of thing. I told her, you can't just toy with people and expect it not to matter. But she never listened."

"This bloke have a name?" Freddie said.

"Kyle Crosby."

"Did you tell the police about him?" Vivian said.

"Yes, I did. He made a scene at a hotel where Joanna was staying and they had to call the police. But then he left before they arrived."

"Do you know where we can find him?"

"I don't know for sure, but this might help," Neville said. She picked up the *El Rio* matchbook and handed it to Vivian. "Joanna gave it to me as a kind of souvenir, I suppose. But it was more than that. She said if anything happened to her this was where Crosby worked as a bartender."

"Thank you for letting us know," Freddie said. "Was there anything else?"

Neville shook her head. "That was it, really. You know everything now." A sad look came into her eyes. "I didn't want to speak ill of her. She was my friend." She looked up at Freddie and Vivian. "Do you think Crosby could've killed her?"

"Passion can be a dangerous thing in the wrong hands," Freddie said. "A chap like that might've thought to himself, if I can't have you, no one else can either."

Neville shuddered. "How awful. If only she'd listened to me."

They left after that. In the car in the way back to the city, Vivian wondered if they'd just added a new suspect to the list.

"What if he did it?"

"Crosby?"

Vivian nodded. We have to find him."

Freddie glanced at her. "Shouldn't you be at work?"

Vivian shook her head. "I got fired."

THIRTY-FOUR

It was the middle of the day and *El Rio* was quiet. The lights were low and a handful of patrons were hunched over their drinks at the long, narrow bar. A lazy country song played on the sound system.

"You ever been here?" Freddie said as they stepped inside.

"Yeah, my ex and I used to come here."

Freddie looked at her. "Your ex?"

"Boyfriend," Vivian said. She winced, as if stung by the memory of the boy who broke her heart.

"What happened, if you don't mind me asking."

Vivian gave a helpless shrug. "He cheated on me."

"I'm sorry."

"Why? It wasn't your fault," Vivian said, a little too sharply.

Freddie looked at her. "You don't take sympathy too well, do you, love?"

A balding, chubby bartender with a blonde ponytail and wearing an Aerosmith T-shirt was watching a game on the flat-screen TV mounted above the bar. He turned to Freddie and Vivian as they slid onto stools.

"Howdy, folks. What can I get you?"

"We're looking for Kyle Crosby," Vivian said.

The bartender shook his head. "Well, I guess you're gonna have to keep looking."

"Why's that?" Freddie said.

"Doesn't work here anymore. I fired his ass a month ago."

Freddie and Vivian exchanged glances.

"Mind telling us why?" Freddie said.

"Who's asking?"

"Freddie Fraser, *San Francisco Sentinel*."

"You a reporter?"

"Crime reporter."

"Kyle in some kind of trouble?"

"Maybe," Vivian said. "Why'd you fire him?"

"He was bad for business. Kept picking fights with the patrons. He'd come to work half-drunk and it got worse from there. I gave him a chance to clean up, but he never took it. Just kept getting into trouble. Got to the point where I'd had enough."

"Got any idea where we can find him?"

The bartender paused, then said, "You might try *Buddha Lounge* in Chinatown. He was working there before. Maybe they were dumb enough to take him back."

Buddha Lounge was on Grant, a narrow street littered with shops and restaurants that served as the main drag through Chinatown. Freddie found parking three blocks away, then he and Vivian headed down the street to the bar. They found it next door to a tea bar and across the street from a gift shop called Heart of Shanghai. The sign above the stylized door frame said "Buddha" in bright red and yellow neon.

Freddie and Vivian walked into the bar and looked around. Tsing Tao paper lanterns cast a dim light on the Chinatown locals, hipsters and tourists drinking their lunches. Vivian noticed a counter with Bruce Lee action figures on sale for $14.99.

A middle-aged Chinese bartender said "What you have?" as they stepped up to the bar.

"We're looking for Kyle Crosby," Vivian said.

"Work nights," the bartender said. "He come in around six."

"Thanks," Freddie said, "we'll be back."

"Where to now?" Vivian said as they headed for the door. Then something caught her eye and she stopped cold.

"What is it?" Freddie said. He followed her line of sight and saw what she saw.

SFPD Homicide Detectives Bassett and Chen were sitting at a romantic table for two in the back of the bar. They were holding hands across the table and looking into each other's eyes.

Vivian's jaw dropped. She looked at Freddie as sheer astonishment spread across his face.

"Blimey," he said. "They're bloody lovebirds."

Bassett looked up and saw Vivian and Freddie. Her eyes widened. She nudged Chen, and then he saw them too. He froze, as if not knowing what else to do. Vivian gave a knowing smile and waved at them. Bassett and Chen exchanged glances, then Bassett stood and walked over to them.

"What are you two doing here?" Bassett said.

"I was about to ask you the same question," Vivian said.

Bassett looked back at Chen, then turned to Vivian.

"It's not what you think," she said, a flustered look on her face.

"Is that on the record, Detective?" Freddie said with a twinkle in his eyes.

"Outside," Bassett said, nodding at the door.

Vivian and Freddie followed Bassett out of the bar.

"Okay, we're outside," Vivian said. "What now?"

"I want you to forget what you saw," Bassett said.

"Excuse me?" Vivian said. "How exactly am I supposed to forget it?"

"Just do it, okay?" Bassett said. "It's between me and Chen and has nothing to do with you."

"Is that also on the record?" Freddie said.

"Um, aren't there rules or something about cops hooking up?" Vivian said. "Just wondering."

"Yes, I do believe the department has policies about fraternization," Freddie said. "Perhaps I should look into it."

Bassett shook her head wearily. "Okay, what do you want?" she said.

"Who says we want anything?" Vivian said.

"So you're just gonna forget it?"

"Let's just say we might develop a case of temporary amnesia."

"In return for what?"

"Simple. You don't hassle us, we don't hassle you," Vivian said. She glanced at Freddie. "Does that cover it?"

"Quite," Freddie said with a nod.

"That's blackmail," Bassett said.

Vivian paused to consider it, then turned to Freddie. "What do you think, Freddie – could we make the six o' clock news?"

"Oh yes, I'll just pop round to the office and write the story. My readers would love to know what the detectives assigned to the Joanna Rorke case are up to in their spare time."

Bassett stared at Freddie. "You're a reporter?"

Freddie smiled politely. "Crime reporter. I'm covering the Joanna Rorke case."

Bassett gave a helpless scowl, then nodded at Vivian. "Let me guess: She's one of your sources."

"Quite," Freddie said.

Bassett shook her head wearily. "Okay, you win... this time."

"Great. Nice doing business with you, Detective," Vivian said.

Bassett turned on her heels and went back into the bar.

"Well, I expect they'll have a bit to talk about now," Freddie said.

"Yeah, and maybe in the meantime they'll leave us alone," Vivian said.

Freddie's phone pinged, alerting him to a text. He pulled out his phone and looked at the screen.

"I have to get back to the office," he said.

"What am I supposed to do?"

A *Murder Tours* bus packed with tourists rolled past them.

Freddie glanced at the bus, then said, "Maybe you could go on a murder tour."

THIRTY-FIVE

Freddie's suggestion reminded Vivian of the *Murder Tours* bus that had passed her apartment building, and how the driver had slowed down and stared at her. She remembered that the driver was the same man who had driven the bus the night of Joanna's reading at Coit Tower. *Why did he do that,* she wondered? *Was he just cruising me, or did it have something to do with Joanna?* She fired up her MacBook when she got home and surfed to the *Murder Tours* website.

The home page was filled with links and information about the various tours the company offered, including lurid photos and descriptions of the crimes that had been committed at the stops on the tour. "See where it happened," the copy promised. "Murder and mayhem on the streets of San Francisco. And you are there." Vivian clicked on "About Us" and was surprised to discover that *Murder Tours Inc.* was run by a man named Floyd Ritter. The page included a photo of Ritter, and Vivian realized she had seen him before. She also remembered that Floyd Ritter was the name on the byline of the manuscript that was on the flash drive Sylvia Torrey had given her. But was it the same Floyd Ritter? Was the man who drove the bus also moonlighting as a mystery writer?

She clicked on "Testimonials" and surfed through comments from happy tourists who talked about how thrilled they were to be at the scene of the crime, and how they couldn't wait to do it again the next time they were in town. The comments all seemed to blend into each other, as if the same person had written them and just used different names to make it seem as if Ritter had dozens of happy customers.

But then Vivian saw two names that stopped her cold: Ben and Sylvia Torrey. They had posted comments about what a great time they had on the tour and how they looked forward to doing it again in the near future. *They knew each other,* Vivian thought. Which meant that the author of the manuscript on the flash drive and the driver of the bus were one and the same: Floyd Ritter. But what did that have to do with Ben and Sylvia Torrey? And why was Ritter's manuscript on Sylvia's flash drive?

Ben Torrey had also posted a comment about how great it was to meet another vintage car guy like himself. Vivian remembered that Ben had apparently gassed himself in his vintage BMW. There was also a message that read "Good luck with *Death Trip.*" Vivian was confused. Sylvia Torrey had accused Joanna of stealing Ben's manuscript, *Tourist Trap,* but where did *Death Trip* fit into the scheme of things. Did Joanna steal that too? And did one of them kill her? Or was it Kyle Crosby?

I guess you could call me and my wife murder junkies. We always go on murder tours when we're on vacation, and Murder Tours was one of the best.

WALT AND CINDY HARRIS, NASHVILLE, TN

THIRTY-SIX

TOM STOOD AT A WHITEBOARD IN THE CENTER OF THE NEWSROOM, surrounded by the entire staff.

"As you can see," he said, pointing at the charts and graphs on the whiteboards, "circulation is going down and costs are going up. Unless we can fix it, we're gonna have to make some adjustments around here." He paused. "Which brings me to buyouts."

A murmur of disapproval rippled through the crowd.

"Just hear me out, okay? Buyouts are better than layoffs, right?"

Freddie's face hardened as he stood by his desk in the back of the room. As far as he was concerned, buyouts were little better than layoffs. In either case, you were out the door. And that was the last thing Freddie wanted. Especially now, when he had hold of a story that any reporter would kill for.

'I just don't want you guys to make the mistake of turning down a buyout and then getting laid off," Tom said. "You know what I'm saying?"

Fat chance of you getting bought out or laid off, Freddie thought as he listened to Tom. As if he cared about anyone except himself and his favorites. Another time he would've thought perhaps he should move on. But not now. The meeting went on a bit longer but Freddie stopped paying attention. He knew the gist of it, the "lede", as they called it around the newsroom, and that was all he needed to know. Tom wrapped up by telling the staff that he would be meeting with everyone personally to discuss opportunities, and then the meeting broke up.

Just then, Freddie's cell phone rang.

"I've got news," Vivian said.

An hour later Vivian and Freddie were sitting on a bench in Yerba Buena Gardens, the lush public park that ran between Third and Fourth and Mission and Folsom Streets. The park was across the street from the San Francisco Museum of Modern Art, and filled with fountains and sculptures. A mix of tourists, office workers taking a break from their cubicles and art lovers wandered through the grounds while panhandlers sprawled on the grass like it was home.

Vivian had her MacBook open on her lap. The Testimonials page on the *Murder Tours Inc.* website was on the screen.

"They knew each other," Vivian said. "They were like friends."

"Yes, quite," Freddie said, reading Ben and Sylvia Torrey's comments. He pulled a Snickers bar out of his pocket, unwrapped it and took a bite.

Vivian glanced at him made a face. "What are you doing?"

"Eating a Snickers bar." He held up the candy bar. "Want a bite?"

Vivian recoiled. "Ewww, no, gross."

Freddie shrugged and took another bite, then said, "But how did three books end up with the same plot?" Freddie said. "Did they steal from each other?"

"I don't know. Sylvia Torrey said that Joanna stole *Tourist Trap* from her husband. But that doesn't make sense because *Death Trip* is the same story. Where does that book fit in? Did Joanna steal that too? Is that why she was killed?"

Freddie ran his hand through his hair. "Blimey, I haven't a clue," he said. "Why would Sylvia be wishing Ritter luck with *Death Trip* when it's the same as *Tourist Trap?*

"What if Ben hadn't yet written *Tourist Trap?*"

"You mean *Death Trip* came first?"

"Maybe."

"And then Joanna's book came last."

"So Joanna stole both of them?"

"Maybe the three of them killed her."

"You're forgetting Kyle Crosby," Freddie said.

Vivian looked at him. "We're on for tonight at Buddha Lounge, right?"

"Yes, the three of us are making a night of it."

"The three of us?"

"Barbara wants to join us."

Vivian's eyes narrowed. "You sure that's a good idea?"

Freddie smiled as he popped the last of the Snickers bar into his mouth. "It's her idea, love, which is all that matters."

"Okay, but there's something I want to do first," Vivian said.

Freddie looked at her. "What's that?"

"I think we should go on a murder tour," Vivian said.

Freddie's eyes widened. "Say what? Go on a tour? Like a bloody tourist?"

Vivian nodded. "I want to get a closer look at Floyd Ritter and the tour is a perfect way to do it. We'll be on the bus with him."

"Crime's my beat, love, remember? I don't need to take a tour to see it."

Vivian smiled. "Come on, you can stand it for an hour or two."

"Yes, I suppose so, but what's the point?"

Vivian shrugged. "I don't know. What if he's the killer?"

"What if he is? He's not going to jolly well announce it, is he?"

"You got a better idea? I want to get close to him. We might learn something."

"All right, then, no harm, I suppose."

"I'll get tickets."

THIRTY-SEVEN

"WELCOME TO THE MURDER TOUR," RITTER SAID AS VIVIAN GAVE HIM their tickets. "I hope you enjoy the ride."

He said it as if he'd said it a thousand times before, and he probably had. Being a tour guide meant you repeated yourself, over and over, day after day. But it did seem to Vivian as if Ritter was speaking only to her. And was it her imagination, or did he linger when he looked at her? The way he lingered when he drove past her house? *Maybe he's just a perv,* Vivian thought. Wouldn't be the first time some creep cruised her.

She had seen Ritter's photograph on the *Murder Tours* website and knew what he looked like. But even without this she would have recognized him as the man she saw sitting behind the wheel of the bus that night at Coit Tower. He was in his late 40s, with a long, hard face and salt-and-pepper stubble. He was wearing a uniform with a *Murder Tours* logo on it. An unlit cigarette dangled from his lips. *He seems like a man born to his work,* Vivian thought, and it gave her an uneasy feeling. And why did she think she'd heard his voice somewhere before? Was that why she suddenly felt trapped as she and Freddie settled into their seats in the front of the bus as the doors hissed shut and Ritter pulled out of the lot?

Ritter kept up a steady patter as the bus rolled past one murder site after another, and after a while they all seemed to blur into each other, a trail of blood and carnage that stretched from end of the city to the other.

"I feel like a bloody tourist," Freddie said.

Vivian grinned. "You are a bloody tourist."

Freddie chuckled.

"Did you cover any of these cases?" Vivian said.

"Some of 'em were before my time, but I covered the rest of 'em. Now they're a bloody tourist attraction." He nodded at the busload of tourists who were busy snapping pics of the murder sites.

"It's San Francisco," Vivian said. "Everything's a tourist attraction."

Then Vivian saw something that made her stiffen.

Freddie must have felt the sudden tension emanating from her body, because he looked at her and said, "You okay, love?"

"Look under the seat," she said.

"The seat? What seat?"

"The driver's seat."

Freddie followed Vivian's line of sight and saw what she had seen: A copy of Joanna Rorke's novel, *The Murder Tour*, was stuffed under the seat.

"Bloody hell, he's reading her book. Quite a coincidence, eh?"

"Yeah, but look at the bookmark," Vivian said.

Freddie craned his neck to get a better look. "Doesn't look like it's a proper bookmark."

Vivian shook her head. "It's not. It's a slip of paper from a hotel notepad." She turned and locked eyes with Freddie. "The hotel where she was killed."

"The Hyatt Regency?"

Vivian nodded. "They're in all the rooms."

"Quite the coincidence indeed," Freddie said.

"What if it's not a coincidence? I wrote down my number on the notepad in Joanna's room."

"What are you saying, it's the same notepad? That's a bit of a stretch, love."

Just then Ritter turned and caught Vivian and Freddie looking at the book stuffed under his seat. A chill ran through Vivian as he gave a grim smile, and she quickly looked away.

THIRTY-EIGHT

BUDDHA LOUNGE WAS ROCKING A NIGHTTIME BAR CROWD WHEN VIVIAN, Freddie and Barbara walked in, a little after ten. Hipsters, tourists and Chinatown locals crowded the bar, shouting orders over the jukebox pumping out 80's pop. Two bartenders, the middle-aged Chinese one with the ponytail Freddie and Vivian had seen earlier in the day, and a younger white man in his 30s, were working opposite ends of the bar and doing their best to keep up with the never-ending stream of orders. The younger man had sandy hair and blue eyes, and he was built like a lifeguard past his prime. He was wearing a Buddha Lounge T-shirt and jeans, and his arms were splashed with tattoos.

"Is that him?" Barbara said, looking at the younger bartender. She was dressed to kill in tight jeans, a halter top and spike heels.

"I hope so," Vivian said.

"He's cute," Barbara said.

A shadow of disapproval fell across Freddie's face. "Mind your manners, love."

Barbara teased a smile. "Jealous, are we?"

Freddie grinned and gave Barbara a squeeze. "Come on, I'll buy you a drink."

"You better," Barbara said.

The three of them made their way through the crowd and went up to the bar. The younger bartender caught sight of them and nodded, as if to indicate that he would get to them when he could. Vivian looked around at the crowd. She hadn't hung out in a bar since she and Jake broke up, and for a moment she wondered if she might spot him in the crowd with Shondra or some other woman. She was relieved when she saw no sign of him.

The bartender came up to them. "What's it gonna be, folks?"

"Got any Guinness?" Freddie said.

"Sorry, pal, got Bud on tap."

"We'll take three pints," Freddie said.

"You mean mugs, don't you?" the bartender said.

"Quite," Freddie said. "My mistake."

The bartender nodded and moved away.

Barbara frowned. "No Guinness? We should've gone back to The Pig & Whistle."

Freddie grinned. He nodded at the bartender. "He doesn't work there, love. That's why we're here."

The bartender returned with three mugs of Bud on tap.

"Thanks," Vivian said.

The bartender nodded and started to move away.

"Kyle Crosby?" Vivian said.

The bartender stopped and looked at her. "Who's asking?"

"We want to talk to you about Joanna Rorke."

Crosby's face tightened. "Who the fuck are you?"

"The press," Vivian said.

"*The San Francisco Sentinel*," Freddie chimed in.

"Fuck off," Crosby said, and moved away. But not before he took a moment to cruise Barbara.

"That went well," Freddie said."

"Yeah, no kidding," Vivian said. "Now what?"

"Maybe he'll talk to me," Barbara said, having noticed the bartender cruising her.

Vivian and Freddie looked at her. "You?"

"Worth a try, love."

Vivian and Freddie watched as Barbara moved down the bar toward the bartender, then slid onto a booth and smiled at him as he poured a mug of draft beer. The bartender returned her smile, then Barbara began chatting him up.

"Oh no," Freddie said.

"What?"

"She's bloody flirting with him."

"Yeah, so? Telling him we're reporters didn't work. Maybe flirting with the guy will work."

"Yes, that's what I'm worried about."

Vivian saw Barbara nod at her and Freddie. The bartender followed her gaze, then shook his head. Barbara covered his hand with hers as she spoke to him. The bartender seemed to reconsider, then nodded. Barbara appeared to thank him, then rejoined Vivian and Freddie.

"He's due for a break in fifteen minutes. He'll talk to you then," she said.

Freddie shook his head. "Still got the touch, don't you?"

Barbara gave a teasing smile. "Think so?"

"What did you tell him?" Vivian said.

"I told him I'd let him buy me a drink if he talked to you."

"What else did you tell him he could do?" Freddie said.

Barbara smiled. "You want to talk to him, don't you?"

Vivian saw a table open up at the other end of the bar. She turned to Freddie and Barbara and cocked her head at the table. "Let's grab it," she said.

Vivian, Freddie and Barbara carried their beer mugs over to the table and sat down.

Freddie looked at Barbara. "You didn't give him the wrong idea, did you?" Freddie said.

Barbara shrugged. "I was just friendly, love, that's all."

"Right," Freddie said. "That's all it takes for some blokes."

"Yeah, especially in a dive bar," Vivian said.

"Look at the two of you, worrying about me," Barbara said. "Do you know how many men have tried to put their hands on me in all the years I've been a flight attendant?"

Fifteen minutes later Vivian saw Crosby approaching the table, a beer mug in his hand.

"Here he comes," she said. She looked at Barbara. "Let's see if coming on to him paid off."

Crosby grabbed an empty chair from another table and sat down. He sipped his beer, then said, "So, what do you want to know about Joanna?"

"You knew her, right?" Freddie said.

Crosby gave Barbara a leering smile. "I did her a couple times, but I wouldn't say I knew her."

"So you were strangers then?" Barbara said.

Crosby shrugged. "I like something strange now and then. She did too."

"We hear you took it hard when she dumped you," Vivian said.

Crosby's face hardened. "Who says she dumped me?"

"That's what we heard," Vivian said.

"You heard wrong."

"We also heard you made a scene at her hotel and the manager called the police." Freddie said.

Crosby scoffed. "Next you're gonna ask me if I killed her."

"Did you?" Freddie said.

"No, but I'm not surprised somebody did, seeing as how she treated people."

"The way she treated you?" Vivian said.

Crosby scowled. "That's none of your business."

"She ever mention a book called *Tourist Trap*?" Vivian said.

Crosby shook his head, then gave Barbara another leering smile. "We didn't talk much, if you follow my drift." He looked at Vivian. "We done here?"

Vivian and Freddie exchanged glances.

"Yeah, I guess so," Vivian said, "unless there's something else you want to tell us about her."

Crosby paused to think about it. "You want me to tell you how good she was?"

Vivian winced. She already knew how good Joanna was.

"We'd rather you didn't," Freddie said, offended that Crosby was willing to share such intimate details, especially about a woman who'd been murdered.

"Okay, then, I guess we're done," Crosby said. He turned to Barbara and smiled. "Let's go outside, baby, just you and me." Then he grabbed her arm and pulled her to her feet.

"Hold on now," Barbara said, taken by surprise. She struggled to break free of him.

Freddie jumped to his feet and moved between Crosby and Barbara. "Let go of her."

"Get the fuck out of my way," Crosby said. He gave Freddie a hard shove and headed for the door with Barbara.

"Hey! Asshole!" Vivian said, trying to pull Crosby away from Barbara. "What do you think you're doing?"

Crosby pushed her out of his way and went outside with Barbara. Freddie and Vivian rushed out after them.

Crosby had Barbara up against the wall. He was groping her and trying to kiss her. Barbara was twisting her head back and forth in a futile attempt to fight him off.

Freddie's face tightened. "Bloody hell!" He went up to Crosby and punched him as hard as he could in the kidneys.

Crosby grunted in surprise. He let go of Barbara and glared at Freddie. Then he delivered a powerful right hook to Freddie's stomach that caused him to double up and sink to his knees.

"Freddie!" Barbara shouted, and moved toward Freddie, who was gasping for breath.

"Where the fuck do you think you're going?" Crosby said, grabbing her by the arm.

Barbara spun around in anger.

"Take your bloody hands off me!" she yelled, then drove a spike heel into Crosby's groin. He cried out in pain as he grabbed his crotch and crumpled on the sidewalk.

"Nice one," Vivian said. The women slapped high fives, then Vivian followed·up with a kick of her own that left Crosby reeling.

Vivian pulled out her cell phone and called 911. She gave the operator the necessary information, then went over to Freddie, who was groaning on the sidewalk.

"You okay?"

"Compared to what?" Freddie said.

"My defender," Barbara said sweetly, and kissed Freddie on the cheek.

Vivian and Barbara helped Freddie to his feet. Vivian glanced at Crosby, who was still moaning on the sidewalk, his hands cupping what was left of his genitals.

Then she heard the sound of sirens.

THIRTY-NINE

A UNIFORM USHERED VIVIAN, FREDDIE AND BARBARA INTO AN interrogation room, then said, "Have a seat, just be a minute."

He walked out of the room, closing the door behind him. Vivian assumed that if she stood and tried to walk out she would discover that the door was locked.

"Are we under arrest?" Barbara said.

"Not yet," Vivian replied, noting that this was her third visit to a police station interrogation room. "But we have a deal, remember?"

"Yes, I remember, but will they?" Freddie said. "But why the devil would they arrest us? We haven't done anything."

Except stick our noses where they don't belong, Vivian thought. Just then the door opened and Detectives Bassett and Chen walked into the room. Vivian noticed that Chen was wearing a mud-colored suit, just like the last two times she saw him. She wondered if he had a closet full of them.

"Hi, Detectives," Vivian said with a wave. "So nice to see you again." She nodded at Freddie. "You remember Freddie Fraser, *San Francisco Sentinel.*" Then she glanced at Chen. "I hope we didn't spoil your date at Buddha Lounge."

Bassett and Chen exchanged nervous glances. She remained by the door as Chen paced the room. Bassett shook her head wearily.

"Here we are again, Ms. Voss. You just can't stay out of a police station, can you?" She nodded at Barbara. "I see you brought company this time. Tell us about your friend."

"Barbara Ridley. I'm a flight attendant."

"You get lost on the way to the airport, Ms. Ridley?"

Barbara's face flushed. Freddie rushed to her defense.

"Barbara's an old friend of mine," Freddie said. "From London."

"London, eh?" Chen said. "You're a long way from home, Ms. Ridley."

"I have a three-day layover in San Francisco. I'm flying out again the day after tomorrow."

"And you thought while you were here it would be fun to play detective, is that right?" Bassett said.

"Hold on now, Freddie said, "she's got nothing to do with it."

"We'll be the judge of that," Chen said. "What were you doing at Buddha Lounge?"

Vivian, Freddie and Barbara looked from one to another.

"What are you looking at each other for?" Bassett said. "It's a simple question."

Vivian took a deep breath, then said, "We wanted to talk to Kyle Crosby."

Bassett and Chen exchanged glances.

"Why?" Chen said.

"We heard that he had a one-night stand with Joanna—"

"Like you, right?" Bassett said with a sneer.

Vivian felt her face get hot. "Yeah, like me," she said quietly.

"So what happened?" Chen said.

"He didn't like it when she dumped him."

"Who'd you hear this from?"

"A friend of Joanna's, Laura Neville."

Bassett and Chen exchanged surprised glances.

"We interviewed her," Bassett said, "she didn't mention him."

Vivian gave a shrug. "She was probably just trying to protect Joanna's reputation." She looked at Bassett. "You arrested him, right?"

Bassett nodded. "We're holding him on a parole violation."

"He tried to assault Barbara outside the bar."

Chen looked at Barbara. "Did you press charges?"

Barbara tossed it off. "We girls dealt with it our way," she said, nodding at Vivian.

"What way was that, Ms. Ridley?"

Barbara stretched out her leg and simulated a kick. "A spike heel where it hurts, Detective," she said, locking eyes with Chen.

Chen got the message and winced. Bassett did her best not to smile.

"Does he have an alibi?" Vivian said. "He could be the killer."

"An alibi?" Bassett said. "Who are you, a homicide detective?"

"Well, does he?"

"No comment," Chen said, glancing at Freddie.

"What about DNA and prints?" Vivian said.

"Just yours and Joanna's," Bassett said. "Whoever murdered Joanna Rorke knew how to cover his tracks."

"Is that on the record?" Freddie said.

Chen looked sharply at Freddie. "This is a police interrogation, Mr. Fraser, not a press conference. You'd do well to remember that."

"Yes, quite," Freddie said. "But it appears you've uncovered evidence that's pertinent to the case, and in my book that's news."

"You guys don't quit, do you?" Chen said.

Freddie smiled politely. "No, as a matter of fact we don't."

"Anything else you want to tell us?" Bassett said.

Vivian paused and thought of Sylvia Torrey. She had told Bassett and Chen about her the first time they interviewed her, right after she'd discovered Joanna's body, when she still had the taste of vomit in her mouth. But at that time Vivian didn't know her name or anything about her. Only that she had asked Joanna about an unpublished manuscript and then thrown a drink in her face. Vivian knew more now, including the fact that Sylvia had motive.

"There's someone else you should know about," she said.

FORTY

"Anything else you want to tell us?" Bassett said.

Vivian looked up at her. She had spent last 20 minutes bracing Bassett and Chen on what she'd learned about the woman who threw a drink in Joanna's face.

"I've told you everything I know," she said.

Which of course wasn't quite true. She hadn't told them about the connection she'd discovered between Ben and Sylvia Torrey and Floyd Ritter. *Why not?* she asked herself. Because she wanted to know more about it, and if she told the police about it she'd never know what they learned. It would be in their hands, not hers, and at the moment Vivian wasn't ready to let go of it.

"What about you?" Chen said, looking at Freddie. "You got anything to add?"

Freddie shook his head. "I think Vivian's covered it."

Chen turned to Barbara. "I don't suppose you have anything to add."

Barbara smiled sweetly. "No, but I must say it is quite exciting to be in the hands of the police. Are you going to arrest us, put us in jail, lock us away forever?"

Bassett and Chen gave each other exasperated glances, then

Bassett turned to Vivian. "Why didn't you come to us the minute you discovered Sylvia Torrey's identity?"

Vivian lowered her eyes.

"Didn't it occur to you that we might want to know, especially as it appears she had motive to murder Joanna Rorke?"

"I don't know. I guess I just got caught up in it, the excitement of it all."

A look of disgust spread across Bassett's face. "I got news for you, little girl. Only amateurs think homicide investigations are exciting."

Barbara frowned. "I say, aren't you being a bit hard on her? If it wasn't for her you wouldn't have known who this woman was."

Bassett and Chen exchanged glances, then Chen looked at Barbara.

"Don't you have a plane to catch?" he said.

"Can we go now, please?" Vivian said.

"What's the rush?" Bassett said. "We were having so much fun."

FORTY-ONE

"WELL, THAT WAS DIFFERENT," BARBARA SAID AS THEY CAME OUT OF THE police station.

It was rush hour and the streets were filled with worker bees heading to their cubicles. *I was one of them*, Vivian thought as she looked around. But that was before Joanna's murder changed everything.

"I must say, I never expected to visit the coppers," Barbara said.

"How'd you like it?" Freddie said.

"It was quite exciting, actually." She looked at Freddie. "Were you afraid they were going to arrest you?"

Freddie chuckled. "Not yet, love. But I don't think they're too happy with us."

"They should be," Vivian said. "They know more now than they did before."

"You mean about that woman, Sylvia Torrey?" Barbara said.

Vivian nodded.

"Do you think she did it?"

Vivian shrugged. "Maybe. But maybe not's good enough."

She knew that Bassett and Chen would track down Sylvia Torrey and bring her in for questioning. But would she reveal the connection between the Torreys and Floyd Ritter? Or the mystery of how three manuscripts, all with the same story, came to exist? Vivian wasn't sure.

"Fancy coffee and a bite to eat?" Barbara said. "I'm starved."

They found a coffee shop a block away and grabbed a table by the window. Freddie and Barbara ordered bacon and eggs and Vivian ordered a bowl of oatmeal with a side of fresh fruit.

Barbara looked at her askance. "Porridge and fruit? That's all you're having?"

Vivian looked at her. "What's porridge?"

"Sorry, that's what we call it in the UK."

"Pay her no mind," Freddie said to Barbara. "She eats like a rabbit."

"Do rabbits eat porridge?" Barbara said.

Freddie cocked his head at Vivian. "See for yourself, love."

Vivian grinned and gave Freddie a playful poke in the ribs.

"About the case," Barbara said, sipping her coffee.

"What about it?" Vivian said.

"Do you think you'll crack it before the coppers?"

"I don't know, maybe we'll get lucky and catch a break."

"Did you always want to be a detective?"

Vivian smiled to herself. She thought about all the mysteries she'd read and how she'd always dreamed about being the amateur sleuth who solved the case. "Yeah, I guess I did. I But I never thought I'd get the chance to do it myself." Then it occurred to Vivian that it took a woman's murder to make it possible.

"The coppers want you to stay out of it. What if you get into trouble?"

We're already in trouble, Vivian thought as she and Freddie exchanged glances.

It matters because I was there, Vivian thought, but was she ready to tell Barbara that she'd spent the night with the murder victim? Then she wondered if perhaps Freddie had already told her.

"I told you, love, I want the story," Freddie said.

"But is it worth the risk, Freddie? I'm worried about you."

Freddie smiled. He reached across the table and took Barbara's hand.

"The story's always worth the risk, love."

Vivian caught the look in Barbara's eyes as Freddie held her hand.

"So what about you two?" Vivian said.

"Us?" Freddie said, tossing a glance at Barbara.

"Yeah, how come you're not together?"

Freddie and Barbara gazed fondly at each other, two old friends who'd once been lovers and yet never quite figured out how to make it stick.

"We're together now," Barbara said.

"Righto," Freddie said. Then his cell phone pinged with a text. He pulled it out of his pocket and looked at the screen, then frowned. "Bloody hell," he said.

"What is it?" Barbara said.

"My editor. He wants a story by noon."

"Still time to see the sights," Barbara said.

Freddie smiled sadly. "Sorry, love."

"But you promised…"

"I'll show you the sights," Vivian said.

Barbara looked at her. "You sure?"

"Sure, soon as I eat my porridge," Vivian said, grinning.

After they'd all finished eating, Freddie and Barbara said goodbye in a long embrace on the sidewalk in front of the coffee shop. Vivian saw that there were tears in Barbara's eyes. She wasn't leaving town yet, but they acted as if she were. Vivian wondered how long they'd carried a torch for each other.

"Cheerio, then," Freddie said. "Happy sightseeing."

"I'll see you later?" Barbara said.

Freddie grinned. "Promise," he said, and kissed Barbara.

Then he hailed a cab and was gone.

FORTY-TWO

"Is that yours?" Barbara said after Vivian had wheeled her motorcycle out of the garage.

"Yeah, it's a Triumph Bonneville T100," Vivian said.

"Triumph? That's a British company, isn't it?"

Vivian nodded. "Yeah, they're still around."

"It's beautiful."

"You like bikes?"

Barbara nodded. "I've never owned one, just ridden on the back holding on to some bloke or other."

Vivian grinned. "Well, hop on and you can hold on to me."

"How exciting," Barbara said as she mounted the bike and threw her arms around Vivian's waist.

"You ready?" Vivian said.

"Quite."

"Hold on," Vivian said, as she revved the engine and roared into traffic.

Barbara screamed with delight as she felt the rush of acceleration.

"You okay?" Vivian shouted over the sound of the engine.

"Yes!"

Vivian headed north on Van Ness, then rode across the Golden

Gate Bridge. The view of the bay dotted with white sailboats was a tourist cliché, but it was still one of Vivian's favorites. When they reached Vista Point on the north side of the bridge Vivian pulled over and killed the engine. Barbara climbed off the bike and looked back at the bridge.

"Blimey, that's beautiful," she said. "You're quite lucky to live here."

Vivian nodded. "You should come more often."

"Yes, I suppose so. It would be nice not to have to wait years to see Freddie again." She turned to Vivian. "Can we ride some more? I'm quite fond of your motorcycle."

They climbed back on the bike and Vivian took Barbara down winding roads in the Marin Headlands, which offered spectacular views of the city, then back across the bridge to Fisherman's Wharf and Pier 39. Vivian parked the bike outside a bar overlooking the water and they went inside and ordered a round of drinks.

"That was quite wonderful, Vivian," Barbara said after they'd placed their order. "I must say I never expected to see the city from the back of a motorcycle."

"Way better than a car, right?" Vivian said.

"Oh my, yes."

The server returned with their drinks. Vivian raised her glass in a toast.

"Here's to you and Freddie."

The toast took Barbara by surprise. She seemed flattered as she smiled and clinked glasses.

"I'll drink to that" she said.

"You never answered my question," Vivian said.

"About why we're not together?"

Vivian nodded.

Barbara sighed. "Oh, I don't know. He wanted to move to the States, I wanted to stay in London. But I suppose it was more than that. Hard to say sometimes why things don't work out even though you want them to."

"I think he was really happy to see you."

Barbara nodded. "I was happy to see him too." She gave a rueful smile. "Perhaps we should give it another go in our old age."

"He's a good guy," Vivian said. "A bit of a slob, though."

"Oh yes. Always has been. I could never get him to clean up. Does it bother you?"

Vivian shrugged. "We're just different, is all."

"Yes, a bit of an odd couple, but here you are, working on a case together."

"I know, funny, huh?"

"I know he's in it for the story, but what are you in it for?"

"Didn't Freddie tell you?"

"Tell me what?"

"Me and Joanna."

Barbara's face flushed. "I don't think he could keep it to himself."

"Yeah, it's that kind of story. Maybe I should tweet about it on Twitter."

Barbara laughed. "It is rather juicy, isn't it?"

"Yeah, except for the part where somebody killed her."

They fell silent. Vivian felt a chill run down her spine. Then Barbara ordered another round, and when it arrived she raised her glass in a toast to Vivian.

"Here's to seeing the city on the back of Vivian's motorbike."

Vivian smiled as they clinked glasses. She hadn't played tour guide in years, not since the last time her parents came to visit. And neither one of them would be caught dead on the back of her Triumph Bonneville. It was way more fun with Barbara, two biker babes on a motorcycle, seeing the sights. But when the sights included a *Murder Tours* bus rolling down the Embarcadero, Vivian felt as if the ghost of Joanna Rorke would always be along for the ride, no matter where she went. Then she remembered seeing Joanna's book with the Hyatt Regency bookmark under the driver's seat when she and Freddie took the tour, and an idea occurred to her.

FORTY-THREE

"What's your favorite murder site, Floyd?"

Ritter looks up at the tourist waiting for an answer. She's an older woman with short, snow-white hair and years in her face, and she's wearing a blue denim skirt and sneakers.

"You must have one you like the best," she persists.

Ritter smiles. They always ask the same questions. Why? Do they think he's an expert on murder? Then again, perhaps he is. Who would know more about the crime scenes than the man who visits them repeatedly, day after day, as if they were shrines. Wasn't that where he got the idea for the book?

"Well," Ritter says, after pretending to give it some thought, "I like this spot right here." He nods at Coit Tower looming in the dark.

"Why's that?"

"Because it's the site of the Zebra Killings," Ritter replies. He remembers that Joanna Rorke had a reading at Coit Tower the night before she was killed. He sees himself sitting in the bus as she read for the last time in her life. That also makes the site special for him. "They cut a woman's head off in a van in the parking lot." Ritter makes a slicing motion with his hand and the woman jumps back, her eyes white with fear. He smiles as the woman looks out at the parking lot and shudders. "It was the beginning…"

"The beginning?" the woman says.

"They took 13 lives, killed 'em execution-style at point-blank range."

"You know a lot about the crime scenes, don't you, Floyd? I guess you would, seeing as how you drive the bus."

"Yep, that's what I do," Ritter replies. "And everywhere I go, people died."

He doesn't tell her that that was how he got the idea. Because then he'd have to tell her the rest of it. And that was out of the question. He looks out at the tourists who've been milling around in the parking lot, snapping iPhone pics of Coit Tower for the folks back home, then honks the horn. Time to go. There are more crime scenes to gawk at, more murders to imagine, more blood to spill.

FORTY-FOUR

FREDDIE WAITED WHILE TOM READ THE STORY FREDDIE HAD SENT HIM. They were sitting in Tom's office, Tom with his back to Freddie while he read the story on his computer screen. Freddie disliked being forced to wait while Tom read his copy, and he thought that Tom sitting with his back turned was rude. He would've preferred that Tom read it alone and then replied to Freddie, preferably by email. But Tom seemed to take pleasure in making his reporters sweat while he reviewed their work. There was something humiliating about it for Freddie, and he wondered if the other reporters in the newsroom felt the same way. Then again, they were younger, and perhaps appreciated Tom's coaching. Freddie did not. Reporters broke the stories that made the news while editors like Tom took the credit.

But Tom's power trip was not the only thing on Freddie's mind. He was also thinking about Barbara, who had suddenly appeared in his life, and was about to leave it just as quickly, a fleeting moment before they'd had a chance to catch up on old times. He found himself wishing she would stay, even though he had no idea what would happen, or whether they could make a go of it again.

His mind wandered to the times they shared in London, when it seemed so easy to be happy together. How would it be now, when they were older and all they had to share were faded memories? *You should never let her go, old boy,* Freddie told himself. Now he could feel time running out. She was about to fly out of his life again, and as he imagined her aboard a jetliner, moving down the aisle as if it were a fashion show runway, Tom spun his chair around and said, "Good copy, Freddie, I like the lede. 'Writer murdered because she stole her bestseller, sources say.' Nice and punchy."

Didn't think I had it in me, did you, Freddie thought. But all he said was "Thanks, Tom."

"You think you can get anybody to go on the record?"

Freddie shook his head. "I'm afraid not. The police said it was strictly off limits."

"Well, keep pushing. I get the feeling there's a lot more to this story."

"Right," Freddie said. *There was much more to the story,* Freddie thought, including the fact that he, Freddie Fraser, was smack in the middle of it. But that was off was off the record, and Freddie had no idea when it would be on the record. Because going public with what he knew could send both he and Vivian to jail for obstruction of justice and interfering with a police investigation.

"There's one other thing I wanted to talk to you about," Tom said.

Freddie waited for the rest of it.

"You know we're talking to everybody about buyouts, right?"

"Yes, I know."

"You interested?"

Freddie shook his head. "No."

"Why not? You've been in the game for a long time, Freddie. Ever feel like maybe it's time to hang it up, do something else?"

"Something else?"

"Yeah, you know, travel, take up a hobby, get out of the rat race?"

"This is all I know, Tom. Wouldn't know what to do without it."

Tom nodded. "Okay, got it. But you're taking a chance because they're talking layoffs, and at least with a buyout you get a package. If you get laid off you get nothing. You understand?"

"Perfectly," Freddie said. "But I must say I'm a bit confused."

"How's that?"

"You like the story but it appears you want me to take a buyout. Which is it, Tom – do you want me to stay or leave?"

Tom gave a tight smile. "I'm just telling you what your options are, Freddie. So you can make the right decision when the time comes."

"I've already made my decision, Tom, so I reckon the ball's in your court now, as you Yanks like to say." Freddie's cell phone rang. "Excuse me," he said, reaching for the phone as he walked out of Tom's office.

"I've got an idea how we can find out more about the connection between Floyd Ritter and Ben and Sylvia Torrey," Vivian said.

FORTY-FIVE

THE KNOCK AT THE DOOR AS SHE HUNG UP WITH FREDDIE TOOK VIVIAN by surprise. She wondered if Hannah had somehow managed to talk her way into the building and was about to abduct her and carry her off to the safety of the suburbs. She wouldn't put it past her. But when Vivian opened the door she saw a husky young man around her age standing there. He was tanned with brown eyes and blonde hair pulled back into a ponytail. He was wearing jeans and a work shirt, and looked as if he spent most of his time outdoors.

"Yes?" Vivian said, in a nervous tone of voice, wondering how he got into the building without using the intercom.

"Vivian?"

"Yeah, who are you?"

The man smiled and stuck out his hand. "Ethan Rorke." He paused for a moment, then said, "Joanna's son."

Vivian was stunned. She stared at Ethan as if he were an apparition. Her legs felt rubbery. The floor seemed to shift beneath her feet.

"Joanna's son?" she said, as if in disbelief, and mechanically shook hands with Ethan.

Ethan nodded. "I wanted to talk to you about my mother."

"What?" Vivian said, as if she'd heard nothing after he said *Joanna's son.*

"The police told me you were the last person to see her alive."

Vivian felt a stab of dread in the pit of her stomach. *What else did they tell you,* she wondered. *That we spent the night together naked in each other's arms?*

Ethan's face creased with concern. "Did I catch you at a bad time?"

Vivian shook her head. "Sorry, I just wasn't expecting anyone."

"Especially me, right?"

Vivian nodded. She managed to collect herself and stepped aside. "Please, come in."

"Thanks," Ethan said, and walked into her apartment.

Vivian closed the door behind him, then indicated the sofa. "Have a seat."

Ethan smiled politely and sat down. "I know this is kind of awkward," he said.

Vivian nodded. "I didn't know. Joanna never said anything about having a son."

"I'm not surprised," Ethan said. "I wasn't really on her radar."

"How'd you find me?"

"The police gave me your name and address. I hope that's okay."

"Yeah, sure, it's just a big surprise is all."

"Yeah, I know."

"But how did you get into the building?"

"The UPS guy left the door open. Sorry, I guess I should've used the intercom."

"It's okay. You want a glass of wine or something?" Vivian said. "I could use one myself."

"Sure," Ethan said with a smile. "Got any beer?"

"Sorry," Vivian said with an apologetic smile.

"No problem, wine would be great. Anything with alcohol, right?"

Vivian went into the kitchen and opened the refrigerator. She pulled out a bottle, then took two glasses out of the cupboard.

"Chardonnay okay?"

"Sure, thanks."

Vivian felt herself relax a bit as she poured two glasses of wine. He was as nervous as she was. She went back into the living room and handed Ethan a glass, then sat down across from him. She was about to say "Cheers," when she realized that since Ethan's visit was about his murdered mother, there was nothing to cheer about. They both fell silent as they sipped their wine, two strangers thrown together by murder.

"So how did you meet my mother?" Ethan said, breaking the silence.

"I went to her reading and she asked me have a drink with her."

Ethan nodded.

"I'm so sorry," Vivian said. "It must have come as a terrible shock to you."

"Yeah, it sure did."

"Do the police have any suspects?" Vivian said, hoping to learn from Ethan what she could not learn from the police.

Ethan shook his head. "If they do, they're not telling me. They just said the investigation was continuing." He gave a wry smile. "I guess they always say that, huh?"

Vivian nodded. "Yeah, I guess so."

Ethan paused. He looked around at Vivian's bookshelves.

"I guess you like to read, huh?"

"Mysteries, mostly," Vivian said.

Ethan gave a rueful smile. "My Mom was a mystery… at least to me." He looked down into his glass. Then he looked up at Vivian. "Can I ask you something?"

"Sure."

"Will you have dinner with me tonight?"

"Dinner?" Vivian said, surprised by Ethan's invitation.

"Sorry, bad idea, huh? It's just that I'm in town for a couple days to take care of things and I don't know anybody here, especially somebody who knew my mother."

"I only knew her for a little while," Vivian said.

Ethan nodded. "I didn't mean to put you on the spot—"

"You like Italian?" Vivian said. "I know a great place in the neighborhood."

If you like murder, you'll love Murder Tours. Forget the cable cars and Fisherman's Wharf and climb aboard the murder bus!

DENNIS BRETT, SAN DIEGO, CA

FORTY-SIX

THE POLICE MUST'VE TOLD HIM, VIVIAN THOUGHT AS ETHAN HELD THE door for her at Carmine's, an old-school Italian restaurant on Polk Street, not far from her apartment. *That's why he asked me out to dinner. Now he's waiting for the right moment to confront me.* Her stomach was in a knot and the thought of eating seemed to make the knot even tighter. Why had she agreed to go to dinner with him? He was Joanna's son – how could she refuse him?

The hostess seated them at a romantic table for two in the back of the room, then lit the candle and handed them menus.

"Thanks," Ethan said after the hostess left them alone.

"For what?"

"Having dinner with me. It's not like you know me or anything."

"Sure, no problem," Vivian said. "You said you wanted to talk about your Mom."

Ethan nodded. "Yeah, I do, except I don't really know what to say. I guess I wanted you to tell me about her, seeing as how you were the last person…" He paused to collect his thoughts. "When I got the call, I couldn't believe it… even now I can't believe it."

He'll never forget me, Vivian thought, *but for all the wrong reasons.*

Whenever he thinks of his mother's death, he'll think of the woman who spent her last night with her.

"We just talked about books and stuff," Vivian said. "She didn't talk about family."

"She liked to pretend she didn't have one," Ethan said.

"That must've been tough for you."

Ethan shrugged. "You get used to it. I used to get a call from her once in a while, but that was about it. I was in Colorado and she was in upstate New York. Sometimes she'd call when she was on tour somewhere."

"Did you ever go to one of her readings?"

Ethan shook his head. "I'm not much into books." He gave a bashful smile. "I'm a carpenter, I build houses. What do I know about books?"

He had a nice smile, Vivian thought, but there was a kind of puzzled sadness in his eyes, as if he was trying to figure out how to grieve for a woman he barely knew who also happened to be his mother.

A waiter came up to the table and told them about the specials, then asked them if they were ready to order, or if they needed more time.

"I'm ready," Vivian said. She looked at Ethan. "You ready?"

Ethan scanned the menu, then set it aside. "I'll have whatever she's having," he said.

Vivian ordered pasta carbonara and red wine. The waiter jotted down the order and moved away from the table.

"You'll love the pasta, it's great," Vivian said.

"Sounds good to me," Ethan said.

When is he going to bring it up? Vivian wondered. The waiter returned with two glasses of wine. Ethan clinked glasses with her and they both sipped their wine.

"I'm not much of a wine drinker, but this is pretty good," Ethan said.

"I'm glad you like it."

Ethan looked around the restaurant. "You come here a lot?"

"Yeah, I guess so."

"I live in a little town you probably never heard of. We've got one Italian restaurant but it's not too good."

"How long are you here for?"

"Just waiting for the coroner to release the body so I can take her back home."

"Where's that?"

"Rhinebeck. It's this kind of arty town in upstate New York. Figured she'd want to be back home. Not that it makes much difference where you are when you're dead, right?"

The waiter returned with their entrees. He set the plates down in front of Vivian and Ethan, then said, "Buon appetito" and moved away.

Ethan smiled as he looked at his entrée, then picked up his fork and began eating.

"Hey, you're right, this is really good," he said.

Vivian smiled. "Great. Glad you like it," she said as she picked at her food.

"I guess I have to confess that one of the reasons I wanted to take you out to dinner is that I just wanted the company. Kinda weird being alone, just waiting around to pick up a body, you know what I mean?"

Vivian nodded. *Maybe he's not going to bring it up*, she thought. *He would have said something by now. Perhaps the police didn't tell him after all.* She took a sip of wine and felt herself starting to relax.

Just then Jake came up to the table. He nodded at Ethan and said, "Who's this, your new boyfriend?"

Vivian looked up at Jake, stunned by his sudden appearance.

"What are you doing here?"

"You don't waste any time, do you, Viv?"

Ethan looked from Jake to Vivian. "Who is this guy?" he said.

"Nobody."

Jake glared at Vivian. "Nobody, huh?" He grabbed Vivian's arm. "You didn't say that when we were together, did you?"

Ethan jumped to his feet. His napkin fell on the floor. He locked eyes with Jake. "Let her go of her."

Jake looked at Ethan and his face hardened. "Stay out of it," he said.

Ethan took a step toward Jake. "I said – let go of her."

Vivian shook free of Jake, then stood and stepped between them. A waiter came up to them.

"Is there a problem?" he said with an Italian accent.

Vivian shook her head. "No, problem." She looked at Jake. "He was just leaving."

Jake scowled at Vivian and Ethan, then pushed past the waiter and headed for the door.

"Sorry," Vivian said to the waiter.

He smiled as if to say all was well now that Jake had left the premises, and moved away from the table.

"Excuse me," Vivian said, "I'll be right back."

She went outside and saw Jake heading down Polk Street.

"Jake!" she shouted.

Jake stopped and looked back to her. "Yeah, what?"

"I want to talk to you."

Jake came up to her. "What do you want to talk about, your new boyfriend?"

"He's not my boyfriend, okay? What are you doing? We broke up, remember?"

Jake said nothing.

"You cheated on me, remember? Or maybe you forgot and you thought I would forget all about it too."

Jake looked down at his shoes. "I didn't forget. I miss you, is all."

"Well, maybe you should've thought of that before you started fooling around with somebody else."

"It was only one time, Viv."

"So I should be grateful?"

Jake shrugged, then nodded at the restaurant. "Who's the guy?"

"Just some guy, Jake, okay?"

"You miss me?"

"You know what, Jake? I got a lot going on, and right now I don't miss anybody."

"Wow. Sounds kinda final, huh?"

"Take care," Vivian said, and walked back into the restaurant.

"Who was that guy?" Ethan said after she sat down.

"My ex," Vivian said, taking a sip of wine.

"I guess he's not too happy you broke up."

"Yeah, well, I wasn't too happy when I found out he was fooling around behind my back."

"I'd never do that."

Vivian looked at Ethan. "No?"

Ethan shook his head. "No, not with a girl like you. A guy would have to be pretty dumb to do that."

Vivian blushed. He was a sweet guy, and for a moment she let herself imagine that she was on a first date that could turn into something more. But then the moment passed. What she and Joanna shared was, as far as Ethan was concerned, her deepest secret. But secrets had a way of being revealed, and Vivian knew she could never live with waiting for the day when he learned the truth. She wasn't ashamed about having had sex with Joanna; she would've done it again if they'd had the chance. But when she thought of it in terms of having had sex with Ethan's mother, it made her feel guilty, as if she'd somehow been unfaithful to him. She knew it didn't make sense, but there was no other way to explain it.

Ethan hailed a cab outside the restaurant after dinner, but Vivian told him she was going to walk home. She needed the space and the cool night air to clear her head. Most of all she needed to be alone before things went any further. Besides, she had other plans.

"You sure?" he said.

Vivian nodded. "It's okay, it's only a few blocks. Thanks for dinner, it was nice."

"I'd like to see you again before I leave."

Vivian paused. "I'm not sure that's a good idea. I'm working through some stuff right now."

"You mean that guy Jake?"

Vivian nodded. Better to let him think it was all about Jake. "Yeah."

"Okay, but I'm around for a couple days if you change your mind."

Vivian leaned in and kissed Ethan on the cheek. "Safe travels," she said, then turned and headed down the street.

She could feel him watching her as she walked away. But then she heard the door slam and the sound of the cab as it pulled away, and she knew he was gone.

FORTY-SEVEN

Freddie buzzed Vivian via her intercom just before midnight and she met him downstairs. She noticed that he wasn't alone. Barbara was along for the ride.

"Hello love," Barbara said as Vivian got in the car. "Out for some fun, are we?"

Vivian closed the door, then turned to Barbara. "This could be dangerous, Barbara. You sure about this?"

"More dangerous than getting groped at 35,000 feet?"

"Yeah, maybe way more dangerous."

"I already told her," Freddie said. "It's no use. She wants to be the getaway driver."

"What?" Vivian said, looking from Freddie to Barbara.

"You know, the wheel man," Barbara said.

"I think you've seen too many movies, Barbara."

Barbara grinned. "It'll be brilliant, love."

"I'm not sure about this plan of yours," Freddie said. He started the car and the engine rumbled into life. "Perhaps we're going a bit too far." He pulled away from the curb.

The car smelled like cigarettes. Vivian made a face and lowered the window.

"I thought you were gonna quit," she said, nodding at the ashtray, which was overflowing.

Freddie waved her off. "Not now, Vivian. I need me fags."

They fell silent. Vivian looked out at the cable car rattling past as it made its last run of the night down the California Street hill. Then she turned to Freddie and said, "Look, I'm not sure about it either. I just thought it might help us figure out how they're all connected. One of 'em did it, or maybe all three of 'em did it, I don't know. You got a better idea?"

"No, I don't. But it's bloody breaking and entering. What if we get caught? It won't be good for either one of us."

Vivian and Freddie exchanged glances.

"Let's just hope we don't get caught, okay?"

"I'll keep the engine running," Barbara said.

"Lovely," Freddie said, glancing at Barbara in the rearview. But the look on his face told Vivian that the caper was against his better judgment.

"Can we go now?" she said.

Freddie started the car. The engine rumbled into life.

"There's something else," Vivian said as they drove down her street.

Freddie glanced at her. "What?"

"Joanna had a son. I had dinner with him tonight."

"Say what? She had a son?"

"The woman who got murdered?" Barbara said.

Vivian nodded. "His name's Ethan. He's in town for a few days, he's taking her back to New York as soon as they release the body."

"How'd he find you?"

"The police gave him my address."

"Did they tell him about you and Joanna?"

"I don't think so. I think he would've said something if he knew, but he didn't. He's a nice guy but it was really weird."

"How so?"

"It was like being on a date, but I never went on a date where I slept with the guy's mother."

Freddie chuckled. "Yes, I expect that must've been a bit strange."

"I'll say," Barbara said. "What if he finds out?"

"Let's hope he doesn't. That would be seriously weird," Vivian said.

Twenty minutes later Freddie pulled up in front of an older, one-story office building south of Market. A sign out front read:

MURDER TOURS!
Visit San Francisco's Most Notorious Crime Scenes!

Tourists were boarding a *Murder Tours* bus parked in a lot next to the building.

"Looks like they're going on a midnight tour," Vivian said.

"To see what – places where murders were committed at midnight?" Barbara said.

Vivian shrugged. "I don't know, maybe."

"A bit gruesome, I'd say."

Just then Vivian saw Ritter emerge from the building, leaving the door open.

"Look, there he is!"

"Ritter?"

"Yeah, that's him. Let's go."

Vivian and Freddie waited until Ritter had boarded the bus, then Freddie grabbed a flashlight from the glove compartment and they got out of the car.

"I'll come round the front," Barbara said. She climbed out of the back and got in behind the wheel. "No worries, love, I'll keep it running," she said, and gunned the engine.

Vivian and Freddie ducked into the shadows, then slipped into the office. There was a row of filing cabinets against one wall and a desk facing windows that looked out onto the parking lot. A laptop rested on the desk.

Vivian rushed over to it before it went dark and was about to start searching it when Freddie whispered, "He's coming back!"

Vivian looked up and saw Ritter walking back to the office.

"Hide!" she said.

Vivian and Freddie looked around in a panic as Ritter approached the office.

"Over there!" she said, pointing to an empty office.

Vivian and Freddie rushed into the office and crouched down behind the door. They heard Ritter enter and then the sound of him settling into his desk chair. Vivian glanced out the door and saw Ritter making notes on his laptop. Then they heard what sounded like a bus horn honking.

"Goddamnit!" Ritter growled to himself.

Vivian peeked out and saw him grab his keys and head for the door. She wondered if one of the passengers had honked the horn just for the fun of it. Vivian watched as Ritter turned the lights off and locked the door behind him, then walked out to the bus. She and Freddie waited until they heard the rattle of the bus's diesel engine, and then the sound of the bus pulling out. Certain that he was gone, Freddie switched on his flashlight and Vivian rushed over to Ritter's laptop and hit a key just as the screen was about to go dark. She looked at Freddie and smiled, then started scrolling through Ritter's emails.

"Hey, look at this," she said.

"What?" Freddie said, looking over her shoulder.

"Emails between Ritter and Sylvia setting up some kind of date."

Freddie looked at her. "She was cheating on Ben with Ritter?"

"Looks that way. Listen to this. 'I really enjoyed our little secret... hope we have more secrets.' It's signed 'S.'"

"I wonder if Ben knew," Freddie said.

"Yeah, I wonder." She looked up at Freddie. "What if Ben didn't kill himself? What if Ritter and Sylvia killed him."

"So they could be together."

"Right."

"But where does Joanna fit in?"

"I don't know. But I want to follow up with Sylvia. She's holding out on us. Let's print this stuff and get out of here."

Just as Vivian sent the emails to the printer a security patrol pulled into the parking lot and stopped in front of the office.

"We got company," Freddie said.

Vivian closed the laptop and Freddie switched off the flashlight.

"Do you think he saw us?" Vivian said as they crouched by Ritter's desk.

She got her answer when she heard the security guard get out of his car and approach the door. She heard him try the door and, finding it locked, the rattle of keys on a key chain and then the sound of the door opening. Vivian's heart was pounding. She felt as if it were about to shatter her ribs and burst out of her chest.

The security guard walked into the office. His flashlight beam swept the room. And then it swept across Vivian.

"On your feet, hands behind your head," the guard said.

Vivian stood and tried to shield her eyes from the guard's flashlight.

"I said hands behind your head!"

Vivian interlaced her hands behind her head. She saw that the guard had a flashlight in one hand and a gun in the other. She wondered where Freddie was and why the guard hadn't seen him.

"What are you doing here?"

"Nothing," Vivian said.

"Right," the guard said. Then he cocked his head toward his lapel mic and said, "Need SFPD backup. Detained an intruder at the *Murder Tours* office on Folsom Street." Then he looked at Vivian. "You alone?"

"Not quite," Freddie said, as he came up behind the guard and hit him hard on the back of the head with his flashlight. The guard grunted and collapsed on the floor.

Freddie looked down at the guard, then smiled, as if pleased with himself.

"Nice one, Freddie," Vivian said.

"Yes, it was, rather," Freddie said.

"The cops are on their way. Let's get out of here."

She grabbed the emails from the printer and they ran out of the office.

FORTY-EIGHT

Vivian and Freddie jumped in the Jag and Barbara pulled away from the office. Freddie was grinning from ear to ear as they raced down empty streets.

"My, that was exciting," he said. "Didn't think I had it in me!"

"I must say I was scared when I saw the guard," Barbara said. "Did he see you?"

Vivian nodded. "He saw me. I would've been arrested if it wasn't for Freddie."

"Why, what happened?" Barbara said, glancing at Vivian in the rearview.

"Freddie knocked him out."

Barbara's eyes widened. "Knocked him out?"

Vivian nodded.

"Oh, I do wish I'd seen that," Barbara said.

Vivian leaned forward and patted Freddie on the shoulder. "Yeah, it was pretty cool how you put him down."

Freddie grinned, pleased with himself. "Yes, it was quite thrilling, I must say."

"My hero," Barbara said, glancing affectionately at Freddie.

"We might not be so lucky next time, you know."

Vivian nodded. "Yeah, but it was worth it. We found out about Sylvia and Ritter."

"Yes, quite, but what does that have to do with Joanna?"

"Maybe Sylvia and Ritter killed her?"

"But what was his motive? She stole Ben's book, not Ritter's."

"That's the part that doesn't add up, because the books are all the same. It doesn't make sense. What do three books with the same story have to do with two deaths?"

"You've lost me," Barbara said.

"I'll explain later, love," Freddie said.

"I want to talk to Sylvia," Vivian said.

"Isn't that a bit risky? What if she calls the police and accuses you of harassing her?"

"She knows more than she's letting on."

Freddie nodded. "So does Ritter, I reckon."

Traffic was light and ten minutes later Barbara pulled up in front of Vivian's building.

Barbara turned to Vivian and Freddie. "So how'd I do?" she said. "I mean as a getaway driver."

Vivian and Freddie shared smiles.

"I'd say you were a right proper getaway driver, love."

"Yeah, you might think about making a career change in case the flight attendant thing doesn't work out," Vivian said.

Then she got out of the car and went into the building. When she got to her apartment she found a note on the door from her landlord reminding her that the rent was past due.

FORTY-NINE

Who was she? What did she want? Floyd Ritter turns on the lights and looks around his office. It's early and he has a little time to himself before the tourists arrive for *Murder in the Morning*, the first tour of the day. But he's rattled by the break-in, and by the calls from the police and the security company. Nothing appears to be missing and yet there has to be a reason why she broke in. The security guard had reported that he was about to handcuff her when someone came up behind him and hit him on the back of the head. *That means there were two of them. Who's the other person?*

He notices that his MacBook is on and that his browser and email app are open, even though he always closes his apps and shuts down his laptop at the end of the day. The emails he exchanged with Sylvia are on the screen. A line from one of them jumps out at him.

I really enjoyed our little secret.

Did she still feel that way? Or did she break in because she wanted to delete the emails and erase all traces of what they had shared? And if it was her, who was with her? He calls her at home.

"Was it you?"

"What are you talking about?"

"Did you break into my office last night?"

"Don't be ridiculous, Floyd. Why would I break into your office?"

"I don't know. Somebody broke in last night."

"Well, it wasn't me, okay?" She pauses. "Why would you think it was me?"

"You sound scared."

"It scares me to talk to you sometimes."

"Because of what happened?"

"I don't know, maybe. Look, I don't have time for this, I have to go to work."

"I'm sorry, I just thought maybe you wanted something."

"What would I want?"

Ritter pauses. *Maybe you've already taken what you wanted?* he thinks.

"I don't know, I'm sorry."

"You're not making sense."

"Somebody broke in."

"I know, you told me."

"But it wasn't you, was it?"

"No."

"It was a woman, though. The security guard saw her."

"I gotta go, Floyd."

The line goes dead. Ritter thinks about the woman who broke into his office. *You almost got caught. That must've scared you. But then look what happened. You got away with it. I can only imagine the adrenaline rush as you escaped. It's exciting to take matters into your own hands, isn't it? But why were you there? Did you want to get on the bus? You missed the midnight tour, but don't worry. You'll be on the bus soon enough.*

FIFTY

Freddie was at his desk at *The San Francisco Sentinel* when reception buzzed him to tell him he had a visitor.

"He says it's important," the receptionist said.

"Be right there, love," Freddie said.

He saved the Word doc on his computer screen, then gulped his coffee, grabbed a notepad and went out to the lobby. The receptionist nodded at an older man in his late 60s sitting in one of the leather chairs by the door. His head was shaved and he was wearing sunglasses and a dark suit that was shiny from too many cleanings.

"You wanted to see me?" Freddie said, coming up to him.

The man stood and took off his sunglasses, revealing sharp blue eyes that had not dimmed with age.

"Freddie Fraser?" the man said.

Freddie nodded. "At your service."

"Eric Haley," the man said, extending his head.

'What can I do for you, Mr. Haley?"

Haley looked around the lobby, then turned to Freddie. "Is there somewhere we can talk?"

"Yes, I suppose so, but what is this in regard to?"

"The Joanna Rorke case," Haley said. "Interested?"

The receptionist gave Haley a visitor's badge and Freddie escorted him to the cafeteria. It was half past nine and the cafeteria was busy with reporters and editors rushing in and out as they fueled up on coffee and pastries before heading back to their cubicles to pound out the day's news. Freddie led Haley to an empty table, then nodded at the coffee machine.

"Fancy a cup?" he said.

Haley shook his head. "I'm good, thanks."

"Splendid," Freddie said, and sat down across from Haley. "About Joanna Rorke…"

"I read your coverage about the case," Haley said. "You mentioned a friend of Rorke's, a woman named Laura Neville."

"Yes, quite. She was supposed to have breakfast with Joanna the morning she was killed."

"You don't know the whole story."

Freddie looked at Haley. "And you do, I presume?"

Haley smiled. "I'm a private investigator, Mr. Fraser. I make it my business to know things."

"And what do you know about Laura Neville?" Freddie said as he began to take notes.

"I worked a case for her a few years back."

"What kind of case?"

"She suspected that her husband was fooling around with someone else – you know how wives are, they've got some kind of sixth sense about these things – and she hired me to keep an eye on him."

Freddie waited for the rest of it.

"It turned out he was cheating on her. Want to guess with who?"

"I haven't a clue," Freddie said.

"Sure, you do," Haley said with a sly smile.

Then it hit Freddie. "Joanna Rorke."

Haley nodded. "The one and only."

"What happened?"

"What usually happens. The lawyers take over and everything goes to hell. One minute you're happily married and the next minute you're picking up the pieces."

"We spoke to her – she never said a word about this. As far as we could tell, she was a dear friend who cared about Joanna and was saddened by her death."

"Well, maybe that's what she wanted you to think. Can't blame her for not wanting to talk about it, can you? But I can tell you she was devastated. The fact that it was her best friend really hit her hard. It was never the same between them after that."

"Why are you telling me all this?"

"I like to see justice done as much as the next person."

"Are you suggesting she murdered Joanna Rorke?"

"I used to be a cop, Mr. Fraser. And when you're a cop everybody's a suspect until they're not."

"So why not go to the police then?"

Haley shrugged. "I try to stay out of their way. Anyway, divorce isn't a crime, and neither is cheating on your spouse or hiring people like me to snoop around. But when I heard about the murder and saw your coverage, I figured a crime reporter like you might be interested in the story behind the story."

"Yes, I am. But I must say it's a bit difficult to imagine her as a suspect."

Haley smiled. "That's the thing about murder; you just never know." He glanced at his watch. "Gotta run."

Freddie escorted Haley back to the lobby. Haley took off his visitor's badge and gave it to the receptionist, then turned to Freddie.

"I hope I haven't wasted your time?" he said.

"Not at all. I had no idea that there might be bad blood between Laura and Joanna."

Haley smiled. "Gives the story a whole new angle, doesn't it?"

"Yes, quite," Freddie said.

"Glad I could help." Haley paused, then said, "You know, the way I see it, your business isn't much different from mine."

"How's that?"

"We both spend our time chasing down leads that we hope will lead to the truth."

"The truth can be rather elusive, Mr. Haley."

"But it's still the truth, isn't it?"

Haley put on his sunglasses and shook hands with Freddie, then turned and headed for the door. Freddie watched him as he walked out of the building. *Haley liked to talk about the truth,* Freddie thought. But he wondered if there was another truth behind his visit, one that had more to do with Haley and less to do with wanting to see justice done.

Freddie went back to his desk and launched Safari, then surfed to the Contra Costa County Superior Court website. He scrolled through divorce records until he found what he was looking for, then he pulled out his cell phone and punched in a number.

FIFTY-ONE

Vivian felt her cell phone vibrate in the pocket of her jeans and nosed the bike to the curb across from a convenience store. Then she took her helmet off, pulled the phone out of her pocket and glanced at the screen.

"I can't talk right now," Vivian said. "I'm on my bike."

"It's important," Freddie said.

Vivian killed the engine. "Okay, what's so important?"

"Laura Neville's been holding out on us."

"What are you talking about?"

While Vivian sat on her bike and the afternoon traffic rushed past, Freddie filled her in on Eric Haley's visit and what he'd learned about Joanna and Laura's relationship.

"She had an affair with Laura's husband?"

"It ended the marriage, according to Haley."

"Do you believe him?"

"It doesn't matter whether I believe him, love. Laura Neville's divorce is a matter of public record."

"How awful for her. Her best friend fooling around behind her back with her husband." Vivian flashed on Jake and how she felt when she discovered he was cheating on her. "She must've been devastated."

"Yes, I imagine she was enraged."

"Enraged enough to kill?"

"Maybe. She had a breakfast date with Joanna, remember? Maybe she had more on her mind than bacon and eggs."

"Why did Haley come to you?"

"He said he wanted to see justice done."

"That means he suspects her of murder. Why didn't he go to the police?"

"Yes, well, that's the part I'm not quite sure about. I'm wondering if this all has something to do with him as well."

"What do you mean?"

"I don't know yet, but one thing's for sure. The number of people who could've had a motive for killing Joanna Rorke keeps growing."

Vivian felt a chill run down her spine. She had spent the night with Joanna while her potential killers lined up outside her door.

"I guess she didn't win any friends, did she?" Vivian said.

"Apparently not, but she was quite good at making enemies."

"So what do we do now? We still need to follow up on Ritter and Sylvia."

"Are you free later? We can meet and sort it out."

"I can't. I'm on my way to my sister Hannah's for dinner," Vivian said, leaving out the part that she had decided to take Hannah up on her offer of rent money. "I'll call you when I get back."

"A bit of the family, eh?" Freddie said.

"Yeah, something like that."

"Brilliant. In the meantime, I'll see what I can come up with on our friend Eric Haley. Cheerio."

Vivian started the engine and pulled out into traffic. She was on her way to the suburbs, where life was supposed to be safer. But the truth was that she no longer felt safe anywhere. Joanna's killer was still out there, and the fact that the list of potential suspects had, in the space of a phone call, grown even longer, only made her more fearful.

FIFTY-TWO

FORTY MINUTES AND TWO FREEWAYS LATER, HAVING LEFT THE CITY FAR behind, Vivian pulled up in front of a ranch-style house with toys on the lawn and a two-car garage. Hannah's SUV was parked in the driveway. It was late afternoon and the sun was throwing shadows on the street. Vivian sighed as she looked at the house. She and Hannah had chosen such different paths, and yet here she was, about to ask for her help. She parked the bike in the driveway behind Hannah's SUV and turned off the engine. Then she locked the bike, slung her helmet over the handlebars and went up to the front door. She could hear the cries of Hannah's boys playing inside, and had to resist a sudden impulse to run back to her bike and ride away. Instead, she rang the bell. Moments later, Hannah opened the door. She saw Vivian and a smile lit up her face.

"Hey sis!" she said brightly.

"Hey you too," Vivian said.

"I'm so glad to see you, honey," Hannah said, and threw her arms around Vivian.

Hannah sure knew how to hug, Vivian thought, as she felt herself being swept up in her sister's embrace. Even when they were kids, a hug from Hannah always comforted Vivian and made her feel as if everything was going to be okay. As they embraced on the doorstep, Vivian felt comforted once again, but she knew it wouldn't last. Too much had happened for her to feel comforted, even though she needed it now more than ever.

Hannah looked past Vivian and saw the bike.

"You rode all the way out here?"

"Yeah, sure, why not?"

"Isn't that dangerous?"

Vivian rolled her eyes. "Oh Hannah…"

"Come on in," Hannah said, "I gotta check dinner or we're never gonna eat."

Vivian walked into the living room and Hannah shut the door behind her.

"I like your outfit," Hannah said, referring to Vivian's black leather motorcycle jacket, jeans and boots. "Very biker."

"Just for you, Hannah," Vivian said, as she looked around the living room. She could hear the shouts of Hannah's sons coming from another room. The smell of Hannah's cooking wafted out from the kitchen.

"Smells good," Vivian said as she took off her jacket and tossed it on the sofa. "What's cooking?"

"Swordfish for you and me. Meatloaf for Dan and the boys."

Vivian looked at her. "You're cooking two dinners?"

"Only 'cause you're here. I knew you'd rather have seafood."

Vivian smiled. "Thanks, Hannah. You remembered."

"Sure, I remembered. Like I'm gonna forget? Least I can do, seeing as how you've come all the way out here to the wilderness. C'mon, you can say hello to the rest of the gang."

Vivian followed Hannah into the den, where Hannah's husband Dan was playing video games with his sons. Dan was around Hannah's age, with an athletic build and sandy hair and blue eyes. Vivian knew that he worked in Silicon Valley, but wasn't quite sure what he did.

Dan looked up at Vivian as she and Hannah walked into the room. "Hey Viv," he said with a quick smile. "Good to see you." He got up from the sofa and gave Vivian a hug.

"Hey Dan," Vivian said. She nodded at the video game playing on the flat-screen TV. "Who's winning?"

Dan made a face and nodded at his sons. "Who do you think? They kick my ass every time."

"Dylan, Wyatt, say hi to Aunt Viv," Hannah said.

"Hi, Aunt Viv," the boys said in unison without taking their eyes off the screen.

"You want a drink?" Hannah said.

"Sure," Vivian said.

"Follow me."

Vivian followed her sister into the kitchen, which was filled with the aroma of cooking. The kitchen was open and airy, and designed for family life. It had gleaming hardwood floors, stainless steel appliances and a dinette table and chairs by the windows, which looked out onto a patio and back yard. There was an island in the middle of the room with all the latest gadgets and above it a skylight that opened the room to natural light. The kitchen reminded Vivian of the pictures she'd seen in home magazines of happy, smiling families hanging out in the kitchen as if it was the center of their lives. And perhaps it was. Hannah's kitchen was about three times the size of Vivian's kitchen, which was actually more of a galley. Then again, she wasn't much of a cook, and wasn't feeding a family.

"Wine okay?" Hannah said as she opened the refrigerator.

"Yeah, sure."

Hannah took out a bottle of Chardonnay and poured two glasses. She handed one to Vivian.

"Cheers, sis," she said, and they clinked glasses.

Vivian sipped her wine, then said, "Anything I can do to help?"

"Yeah, you can keep me company," Hannah said. "I'm usually in here by myself."

"Dan helps, doesn't he?"

Hannah shrugged. "Yeah, when Dylan and Wyatt let him. They run the place, you know."

They shared a smile, then Hannah turned serious.

"You get any more threatening phone calls?"

Vivian shook her head.

"You report it to the police?"

Vivian shook her head again.

"Why not?"

Vivian looked at her sister, then looked away.

You're not still playing detective, are you?" Hannah said.

"I'm not exactly playing, Hannah."

"What do you call it then?"

Vivian sipped her wine and said nothing. What could she say? Hannah would never understand. Vivian scarcely understood it herself.

"Why is it so damn important to you?"

Vivian shrugged. "I was with her."

"So you were with her. So what? Why does that mean you have to put your life in danger?"

"I guess I just need to know, and I don't want to wait for the cops or anybody to figure it out. I want to figure it out, okay?"

Hannah sighed. "You're not gonna give it up, are you?"

Vivian smiled. "I'm on the case, sis."

"You're on the case. Great. You know what, Viv? Maybe you should've been a cop instead of a copywriter."

"Maybe you're right," Vivian said as she sipped her wine. "It's way more fun."

"Speaking of copywriting, how's the job search going?"

"That's what I wanted to talk to you about."

"You need money for the rent?"

Vivian nodded. She felt the color rush into her face. Asking her sister or anyone else for money was the last thing she wanted to do. She prided herself on her independence, but it was hard to be independent without a paycheck.

"I hate to ask, Hannah—"

"Don't worry about it, okay? I'm worried enough about you already. I don't need to be worried about you being out on the street."

"Thanks. I'll pay you back."

"You can pay me back by staying out of trouble."

Just then Dan and the boys burst into the kitchen.

"When are we gonna eat, Mom?" Dylan said.

"I'm hungry," Wyatt said.

Dan smiled. "Nothing like video games to work up an appetite."

Hannah rolled her eyes. "Guy stuff." She looked at Vivian. "You want to help me set the table?"

"Sure," Vivian said, grateful for something to do, and began taking out the plates and glasses and silverware they would need for dinner.

"Remember when we had to do this when we were kids?" Hannah said.

"Yeah , it was our job."

"You know what? You get married and it's still your job," Hannah said. Then she went to the doorway leading to the living room and called out to her family. "Dinner's ready. Let's go, guys."

Moments later, Dan and the boys made their way from the den to the teak dining room table that Vivian knew had come from Design Within Reach.

"So how's work?" Dan asked as they began eating. "You still at the same agency?"

Vivian shook her head. "I got laid off," Vivian said. She threw a quick glance at Hannah, as if to say, *Leave it at that.*

"Sorry to hear it," Dan said. "You want me to look around at my company? I could check with Marketing and see if they need a writer."

"That's okay. I want to stay in town."

"I don't blame you for not wanting to commute. It's a bitch and it's getting worse every day."

"I'm sure you'll find something soon," Hannah said. "Agencies always need copywriters, right?"

Vivian smiled. "Yeah, I'm not worried."

"Can we go eat in the other room?" Dylan said.

"Yeah, we want to keep playing," Wyatt said.

Dan smiled and shook his head.

"No, you may not keep playing," Hannah said. "We're a family and families eat together."

Dylan and Wyatt exchanged sullen glances as they picked at their food.

"And no pouting either," Hannah said.

Family life, Vivian thought. This was what it was like. As she watched Hannah with her husband and sons, she tried to imagine what it would be like to have a family of her own. But it was impossible to picture it. Maybe it took meeting the right guy to be able to see a future together that came with a house in the suburbs, fancy kitchens, a two-car garage and toys on the lawn. Vivian felt far from that now, further than she could have ever imagined. Joanna Rorke had changed everything, and even in death continued to haunt her.

"You want to stay overnight instead of having to drive back to the city?" Hannah said after they'd cleared the table and filled the dishwasher.

Vivian shook her head. "I'm gonna go home."

"You sure? It's a long way to go in the dark."

"I'm a big girl, Hannah, I think I can handle it."

"Yeah, that's what I'm worried about."

Vivian leaned in and hugged her sister. "Thanks, sis. This was fun."

Hannah tried to smile, but Vivian could see the worry in her eyes.

"It's gonna be okay, Hannah, honest."

"She's dead, Viv. Let her go and move on."

"That's what I'm doing, Hannah. I'm moving on, maybe for the first time in my life."

FIFTY-THREE

As Vivian emerged from the Bay Bridge tunnel at somewhere north of the speed limit, the San Francisco skyline appeared before her. It was one of her favorite views of the city, and it was even better at night, when the town seemed to sparkle in the lights like a mirage. Riding a motorcycle at night was always more dangerous than riding in daylight, but Vivian loved the feel of the bike beneath her and the roar of the engine in her ears as she shot through the dark under a starlit sky. Best of all, though, the view made Vivian feel as if she was home.

There was a police car parked in front of her building. Vivian felt her stomach tighten. She'd had her fill of cops since Joanna was murdered, and the sight of the black and white cruiser made her tense. Then she wondered if somebody else's apartment had been broken into. But as she pulled up in front of the garage, two uniformed police officers stepped out of the black-and-white cruiser and came up to her.

"Vivian Voss?" the first cop said. He had blonde hair and looked hot in his uniform.

"Yes, why?"

"You need to come with us," the second cop said. He was black with a mustache and goatee, and looked like he worked out.

"What are you talking about, what's going on?" Vivian said as the panic climbed into her throat.

The black cop pulled out a pair of handcuffs.

"Step off the bike."

"Can I put it away…please?" she said. "I can't just leave it on the street. It'll get stolen."

The two cops exchange glances, then the white cop said, "Okay, make it fast."

Vivian pulled out a remote and used it to open the garage door. The cops followed her as she rode the bike into the garage, then parked and locked it.

"Let's go," the black cop said.

The cops led Vivian out of the garage. She used the remote to close the garage, then the black cop took her by the arm and cuffed her hands behind her back.

"That hurts!" Vivian said, trying to wriggle free. "What are you doing?"

The cops led Vivian to the cruiser and put her in the back seat. *Here I am again, in the back of a police car,* Vivian thought as the cruiser flashed down nighttime streets.

"Am I under arrest? You didn't read me my rights." Vivian said. "Aren't you supposed to do that?"

She saw the driver glance in the rearview. Her mind raced as she tried to imagine why she'd been taken into custody. *What did they know?* she wondered. *What do they think I've done?*

When they reached the police station the cops escorted Vivian into an interrogation room, then left her alone. Moments later, Bassett and Chen walked into the room. Vivian looked up at them.

"Well, if it isn't the happy couple," she said.

"Well, here we are again, Ms. Voss," Bassett said.

"Don't you guys ever go home?" Vivian said. "You want to tell me what's going on?"

"We're hoping you could tell us," Chen said.

"What are you talking about?"

"There was a break-in at the *Murder Tours* offices south of Market the night before last."

Vivian flashed on Ritter's office. *Nobody saw us,* she thought. Then she remembered the security guard.

"What's that got to do with me?"

"You tell us. You were on a *Murder Tours* bus the night Joanna Rorke was killed."

Vivian scoffed. "Right. So I rode the bus and then I broke into the office. What was I looking for, souvenirs?"

"Could be," Chen said. "That's why you're here."

"Before somebody clubbed him and knocked him out, the security guard said he saw a young woman who fits your description," Bassett said.

"A lot of women look like me," Vivian said.

"Maybe," Chen said with a shrug. "That's why we're gonna do a lineup."

Vivian looked at him with a puzzled expression. "Excuse me?"

"A lineup. You and four other women who look like you."

"What if I say no?"

"That's the thing – you can't," Bassett said.

"Wait a minute," Vivian said, "I thought we had a deal."

Bassett and Chen exchanged glances.

"You don't hassle me and I don't hassle you, remember?"

"I got no choice," Bassett said. "You fit the description, so we gotta do the drill."

Bassett escorted Vivian to a holding cell with four other slender brunettes in their 20s. All of them were roughly the same height and weight as Vivian, and had similar hair and skin color. The women looked up at Vivian with amused expressions as Bassett locked the cell door behind her and moved away.

"Welcome to the lineup," the first woman said. "Say hello to the suspect, girls."

"Excuse me?" Vivian said.

The woman looked around at the others in the cell. "We're fillers, which means you're the suspect."

"I don't understand. What are you talking about?" Vivian said.

"We get paid ten bucks to fill out a lineup," the second woman said. "You need at least five people for a lineup – the suspect and four fillers."

"It's kind of a cops and robbers version of central casting," the third woman said.

"Whenever they need to pull somebody in for a lineup, they pull in people who match the suspect's description," the fourth woman said. "Simple, huh?"

"Yeah, simple," Vivian said in a dejected tone of voice as she slumped on a bench.

"Your first time, huh?" the first woman said.

Vivian nodded.

"What's the charge?" the second woman said.

"Breaking and entering," Vivian said.

"But you didn't do it, right?" the third woman said with a teasing smile.

Just then, Bassett came up to the cell and unlocked the door.

"Showtime, girls," she said.

Vivian and the four other brunettes walked out single file onto a scuffed platform wearing numbers. Vivian was Number 2. There was a two-way mirror in front of them and a height chart behind them. The chart started at three feet and ran to seven, which Vivian figured would cover most people, except maybe basketball players.

"Okay, line up," a police voice barked. "When your number's called, take a step forward. No talking."

When her turn came Vivian took a step forward and stared at the mirror. She pictured the security guard staring at her and trying to determine whether she was the woman he saw in the glare of the flashlight before the lights went out. She felt mortified and embarrassed by the attention, people staring at her as if she was an animal at the zoo. She was also terrified that the security guard would turn to Bassett and Chen and say, *Yeah, that's her.*

A moment later she was told to step back and the show moved on to the other women on the stage. When it was over Vivian was escorted back to the interrogation room. Five minutes later, Bassett and Chen joined her.

"Okay, you're free to go," Bassett said.

Vivian looked at her. "Seriously? That's it?" she said. "This is the second time you've dragged me in here in handcuffs."

"We apologize for any inconvenience," Bassett said, ice in her voice.

"Your witness couldn't identify me, right?"

"Yeah, that's right," Chen said.

"Maybe 'cause I was never there," Vivian lied.

"I think you were there," Bassett said.

"You just can't prove it."

Bassett glanced at Chen, but said nothing.

"Sorry to disappoint you," Vivian said as she stood and headed for the door. "But if you ever need a filler, give me a call. I just lost my job and I could use the money."

FIFTY-FOUR

ERIC HALEY HAD TOLD FREDDIE ALL ABOUT LAURA NEVILLE'S relationship with Joanna Rorke, and filled him in on Joanna's role in breaking up Neville's marriage. But he had left out the juicy bits. Which of course were the bits that Freddie was most interested in. Betsy Woodruff, who worked in the Records Unit of the San Francisco Police Department, braced him on what Haley had kept to himself. They were sitting in her office on the first floor of the new SFPD headquarters building on 3rd Street in the Mission Bay district.

"He tried to blackmail her husband," Woodruff said, cutting to the chase.

She was chubby woman in in her 50s, with a round face and long gray hair that she wore in a ponytail. Glasses were slung on a lanyard around her neck. There was a cat calendar on the wall behind her, and framed photographs of her cats on her desk. Woodruff had worked for the SFPD for as long as Freddie had been at the *Sentinel*, and their mutual love of cats had always made Freddie feel as though they belonged to the same tribe.

Freddie stared at her. "Haley?"

Woodruff nodded.

"Bloody hell. He was a private eye. How the devil did he turn into a blackmailer?"

"When he found out that Laura's husband was fooling around, Haley approached him and offered him a deal."

"What kind of deal?"

"For a price, he would tell Laura that he had found no evidence that her husband –I believe his name was Philip – was cheating on her."

Freddie chuckled. "Got a bit greedy, eh?"

"He saw a chance to cash in and went for it."

"Did he think Philip would go for it?"

"Apparently, but there was just one problem."

"Philip pushed back."

Woodruff nodded. "He filed for divorce and accused Laura of hiring Haley to blackmail him. Laura had done no such thing, of course, and the whole thing came as quite a shock to her. As did the fact that Philip was having an affair with her best friend."

"What happened to Haley?"

"Laura reported the attempted blackmail and Haley lost his license. I have no idea what he's doing now." She looked at Freddie. "Why are you asking about him? Is it because of the Joanna Rorke murder case?"

"Haley came round to see me the other day. He knew I was covering the case and wanted to tell me about Joanna's affair with Laura's husband. But he *didn't* tell me that he tried to blackmail her husband."

"No, he wouldn't, would he?"

"I thought there might be more to it than just the affair."

"Which is why you came to see me."

"Quite."

"Well, that's all I know, Freddie. It didn't end well for any of them. Especially Joanna, of course."

"What happened to Philip and Joanna?"

Woodruff scoffed. "There was no Philip and Joanna after that.

From what I heard, she dumped him when it all hit the fan. He pretty much disappeared after that."

"Yes, I gather she wasn't one to stick around when things went south."

Freddie paused. Woodruff looked at him.

"What is it?"

"Why would Haley dredge this all up now? He must've known I'd find out about the blackmail."

"Bad blood between him and Laura, maybe. It never quite goes away, you know."

Freddie nodded. "Yes, I suppose so." He gave Woodruff a grateful smile. "Thanks for your time, love, I appreciate it."

"Anytime, Freddie. How are your babies?"

Freddie smiled. "Nigel and Claire?"

Woodruff nodded.

"They're me life." He pulled out his cell phone and showed Woodruff pics of his cats.

A tender smile softened Woodruff's face as she looked at the pics. "They're lovely, Freddie."

Freddie beamed like a proud parent. "Thanks, love." He nodded at the cat photos on Woodruff's desk. "And yours?"

Woodruff shrugged. "The same, of course. Don't know where I'd be without 'em."

They shared an understanding smile, and then it was time to go. Freddie waited until he'd walked out of the building, then pulled out his cell phone, launched Safari and searched for a name.

FIFTY-FIVE

HALEY'S OFFICE WAS IN A RUNDOWN PILE SOUTH OF MARKET, JUST DOWN the road from the SFPD's Bryant Street jail. According to the directory in the lobby of the building, which also housed a bail bondsman called *Bad Boy Bail Bonds*, Haley was on the second floor. Freddie took the elevator. He had thought about calling ahead, then decided it was best to just stop by and surprise Haley. He didn't want to give him another chance to hold out on him.

The elevator shuddered to a stop on the second floor. The doors slid open. Freddie stepped out and headed down the corridor. He noticed that the walls were scuffed and needed repainting and the carpet was faded and threadbare. He wondered what Haley's game was now, given that he'd lost his license to practice as a private investigator. Was he working in some capacity with the bail bonds office downstairs, or was it just a coincidence that their offices were in the same building?

A receptionist looked up at Freddie as he stepped into the cramped office. She was skinny and in her 40s, and had a pale complexion, as if she'd spent too much time indoors. The gang tattoos on her neck made Freddie wonder if she'd been in prison.

"May I help you?"

Freddie nodded at the closed office door behind her. "Is he in?"

"Who's asking?"

"Freddie Fraser, at your service."

The receptionist looked at Freddie skeptically. "Do you have an appointment?"

Freddie gave an apologetic smile. "Sorry."

The receptionist pressed a button on her phone. Freddie heard Haley say, "Yes?"

"There's some guy named Freddie Fraser here to see you," the receptionist said.

There was a pause, then Freddie heard Haley say, "Send him in."

The receptionist looked up at Freddie. "You heard him," she said.

"Quite," Freddie said with a polite smile, then moved past her desk toward Haley's office.

Haley looked up at Freddie with a puzzled expression as he stepped into the office.

"Freddie Fraser," he said. "What a surprise."

The look on his face told Freddie that Haley didn't especially appreciate surprises.

"Yes, quite," Freddie said.

"What can I do for you?"

"Just a bit of follow-up, if you don't mind."

Haley checked his watch. "Sure, why not. I can spare a few minutes."

"Lovely, thanks so much," Freddie said, and closed the door behind him.

"Have a seat," Haley said, indicating one of the two chairs facing his desk.

Freddie smiled politely and sat down. The office was the size of a closet, and had just enough room for a desk, a few chairs and a couple of dusty filing cabinets.

"So…what's this all about? I told you all I know."

"Not quite," Freddie said.

"What'd I leave out?"

"Well, it's a bit awkward, but you didn't tell me about the blackmail."

Haley's face tightened. "Who told you about that? One of your sources?"

Freddie looked at him. "Why didn't you tell me about it?"

"I didn't think it was any of your business."

"Yes, well, you see, it *is* my business because it's part of the story."

"Okay, so now you know. So what? It doesn't change anything. Laura Neville had a motive to kill Joanna Rorke. That's the story and you know it."

"Well, you may be right, but—"

"Damn right I'm right."

"But why did you do it?"

Haley paused. He stood and walked to the window, which looked out on the building next door.

"I saw an opportunity," he said, looking out the window.

"But it was a crime."

Haley turned and looked at Freddie. "Crime's an opportunity, isn't it?"

Freddie shrugged. "Yes, I suppose it is, unless you get caught."

"Yeah, well, I got caught and I paid the price," Haley said. He scowled at Freddie. "Is that what you came here for, to humiliate me?"

Freddie shook his head. "I'm a reporter, Mr. Haley. All I want is the story."

"And I suppose that now you think you've got it."

"You tell me," Freddie said.

"Did you talk to her about it?"

"Laura?"

Haley nodded.

"Not about this, no."

"Well, then, you don't have the whole story, do you?"

Freddie looked up at Haley. "Say what?"

"She was in on it," Haley said.

Freddie stared at Haley. "Excuse me?"

"Who was in on it?"

197

"The blackmail. It was Laura's idea."

Freddie was stunned. According to Betsy Woodruff, Laura knew nothing about Haley's attempt to shake down her husband. And yet here was Haley telling him that she was. Freddie wondered what was true, or if any of it was true.

"I don't understand…"

"She wanted to punish Philip by bleeding him dry financially. She figured he'd pay me off to keep his affair under wraps and I'd get a piece of the action."

"But it didn't work out that way, did it?"

Haley shook his head. "He wasn't gonna give me a dime, even if it meant going public with the affair and destroying his marriage. What he didn't know was that Laura had already decided to divorce him."

"I thought you said *he* filed for divorce."

Haley shrugged. "They divorced each other."

Freddie took a moment to let the news sink in. "Bloody hell, that's quite a story."

"Yeah, and now you've got it, all of it. So you can get the hell out of here."

Freddie nodded. He stood and walked to the door.

"One more thing," Haley said.

Freddie turned to him. "Yes?"

Haley looked around his dingy office. "I wasn't always like this," he said.

Freddie gave an understanding smile. *The same could be said of most of us*, he thought. *Life's a game and the dealer's a joker.* He walked out of Haley's office, closing the door behind him.

When he got back to the Jag there was a parking ticket under the windshield. He scowled. "Bollocks," he muttered under his breath. He grabbed the ticket and crumpled it in his fist, then unlocked the door on the driver's side and slid in behind the wheel. He opened the glove compartment, which was stuffed with parking tickets, candy wrappers and receipts, added the ticket to the pile and closed the compartment.

He reached in his pocket for a cigarette, lit it and pulled the smoke down into his lungs. Freddie knew he should quit; he was reminded of that fact every time he lit up. But how could he quit now, after so many years? Even now he could remember nicking smokes on London streets as a lad. At least Vivian wasn't in the car and he could steal a smoke in peace. It was sweet of her to care about his health. Perhaps she cared about it more than he did. But for the moment, all Freddie wanted to do was give himself time to think, and nothing gave you time to think like a cigarette.

Everything in the case seemed to be turning into something else, and whatever he thought was the truth became a different truth, which might in turn become another truth as he learned more about the case. Joanna Rorke had gone from being Laura Neville's friend to a woman who cheated with her husband behind her back and destroyed Laura's marriage. And Laura herself had gone from being Joanna's friend to a woman who had a motive for murdering her. And as if that wasn't enough, Laura had tried to use Joanna's betrayal to blackmail her philandering husband. In the process, Eric Haley, the PI who played along for a payoff, lost his license and destroyed his career. Freddie rubbed his eyes as the plotlines kept unfolding, doubling back on each other and taunting him, as if to say, that whatever he had thought was right was wrong.

He could hear the traffic rushing past him. *Time to go,* he told himself. He reached for his cell phone and punched in a number.

"I have news, love," he said.

Murder Tours puts you at the scene of the crime, and makes you feel as if you were the killer. We really like that!

MARK AND STEPHANIE ATKINS, LAS VEGAS, NV

FIFTY-SIX

SYLVIA WAITS. SHE HAS NO CHOICE. SHE HAS TO GET IT BACK. THIS IS her last chance. And so she'll wait for as long as it takes. She's waited before. It's no big deal, she knows what it's like. She remembers how she waited at the hospital for news about Ben, even though she knew he was already dead. She was waiting for nothing then, because he was already gone. Even so, she couldn't stop waiting. She waited because she didn't know what else to do.

It's different now. She's waiting for something that matters. Her life depends on it. People say that all the time but it's true. Her life really does depend on it. She needs to get it back before he finds her, because by then it'll be too late. *It was too late for Ben, but it's not too late for me,* Sylvia thinks. *I'll go away,* she tells herself, *I'll be somebody else. People do it all the time.*

She looks around the room. So different from where she lives now. Nicer too. Everything in its place, as if the person who lives there knows where everything belongs. Maybe even knows where she belongs. *That's the important thing,* Sylvia thinks, *to know where you belong.* She doesn't know where she belongs anymore. She used to think she belonged with Ben, and wherever they were was her place in the world.

Maybe she should've been in the car with him when he gassed himself. Maybe that was where she belonged. But he didn't warn her ahead of time. He didn't call her at Safeway and tell her he was going to fill his lungs with carbon monoxide. He just let her find him in the garage when she came off a twelve-hour shift at the Safeway in Concord. Her husband. The man who told her they'd always be together no matter what. But they weren't together when he dangled the garden hose through the window and started the engine.

She's moved around since then. Safeway keeps transferring her to different stores and sometimes she has to move because the commute is too much for her. She knows where she lives now is a dump, but that's even not the worst part. The worst part is that he knows where she lives.

She wonders how long she'll have to wait. The thing in her hand is heavy and she's tired of holding it. She goes into the kitchen and opens the refrigerator. She finds a bottle of white wine and pours herself a glass. But she doesn't pour just a little, the way they do in fancy restaurants. She's not in a fancy restaurant, and so she fills the glass to the brim and takes a sip. Then she takes another. Depending on how long she has to wait she might drink the whole bottle. So what? Nobody's waiting for her at home. Nobody's going to tell her that she's drinking too much or that drinking and driving is dangerous. Everything's dangerous in her life now. Which is why all she can do is wait and hope that she's not waiting to die.

FIFTY-SEVEN

FREDDIE WAS STANDING OUTSIDE *THE SAN FRANCISCO SENTINEL* building when Vivian rode up on her motorcycle.

"What happened to the Jag?" she said.

"Bloody car won't start." Freddie nodded at the bike. "What's that?"

"It's a Triumph Bonneville," Vivian said. "It's from the UK, just like you, Freddie."

"Where's your car?"

"I don't have one."

Freddie's jaw dropped. He looked at Vivian with disbelief. "You mean you want to me to ride on that?"

"Only way we're gonna get there, Freddie."

Freddie hesitated. "Is it safe?"

Vivian scoffed. "Duh. It's a motorcycle, dude."

"Bloody hell," Freddie said, and climbed onto the bike.

"Hold on to me," Vivian said, "and don't let go."

Freddie threw his arms around Vivian's waist and held on for dear life.

"You ready?" Vivian said.

She twisted the throttle. The bike sped away from the curb. Freddie let out a cry as Vivian merged into traffic, then headed toward the Bay Bridge and Contra Costa County. Thirty minutes later she pulled up in front of Laura Neville's condo in Walnut Creek.

"You okay back there?" she said.

"Yes, it was quite thrilling really," Freddie said. He looked out at the condo. "I reckon she won't like seeing us again."

"Yeah, especially when we ask her about the blackmail."

They climbed off the bike and went up to the front door. It opened before they had a chance to ring the doorbell. Vivian figured the roar of the bike must have alerted Neville to the fact that she had company.

"Hi…" she said. A look of surprise swept across her face. "What are you doing here?"

"I apologize for not calling ahead," Vivian said.

"May we come in?" Freddie said.

"Not until I know why you're here," Neville said, arms folded, blocking the door. "I've already told you all I know."

Vivian and Freddie exchanged glances, then Freddie said, "I spoke to Eric Haley, Laura. We know about the affair."

"And the blackmail," Vivian said.

The color drained out of Neville's face. Her arms dropped to her sides. She stared at Vivian and Freddie with a shocked expression.

"May we come in?" Freddie said again.

Neville hesitated for a moment, as if she hadn't heard Freddie, then stepped away from the doorway. Vivian and Freddie slipped past her and went inside. She closed the door, then turned to Vivian and Freddie, who were standing in the living room.

"What did Haley tell you?"

"Maybe we could all sit down," Vivian said.

"Yes, of course," Neville said. "Please, sit down."

Freddie smiled politely, then he and Vivian sat in the club chairs facing the door. Neville walked over to the sofa and sat down across from them.

"Would either of you like a drink?" she asked.

"I'm good," Vivian said.

"It's a bit early for me," Freddie said.

"I wish I could say the same," Neville said. "Excuse me."

She stood and went into the kitchen. Vivian heard the tinkle of ice cubes in a glass, then Neville walked back into the living room with a drink in her hand. She took a sip, then sat down again.

"So what did he tell you?" she said.

"He told us about Joanna and your husband," Freddie said. "He said you tried to blackmail him."

"Is that true?" Vivian said.

Neville took another sip, then set her glass down a little harder than she needed to on the coffee table.

"Yes, it's true."

"Why didn't you tell us?"

Neville looked sharply at Vivian. "Would you want to talk about it if it was your best friend and your husband?"

"Why did you try to blackmail him?" Freddie said. "Haley said it was your idea."

Neville nodded. "I wanted to hurt the bastard, just like he hurt me." She smiled bitterly. "Joanna was my friend, my dear friend, and she was fucking him behind my back. I thought Phil and I were going to spend the rest of our lives together..." Her voice trailed off and she reached for her drink.

"I know how that feels," Vivian said, thinking of how she felt when she discovered that Jake was cheating on her. "But you made it seem as if you were still friends... you were going to have breakfast with her the morning she was killed..."

Neville nodded, then took another sip. "It doesn't make sense, does it. But I was lonely after Phil and I split up, and I missed her. I missed her being my friend."

"Forgive me for saying so, but one could say that you had a motive for killing her."

"Yeah, I suppose I did. And there were times when I wished she was dead." She looked sharply at Freddie. "But I didn't kill her, if that's what you're getting at. I don't own a gun and wouldn't know how to use one if I did."

"So what happened?" Vivian said. "How did things change between you and Joanna?"

"She wrote to me, apologizing for what had happened. I threw her letter away, but then she wrote again, and this time I wrote back. She said she was going to be in town, and that she hoped we could meet, that she missed our friendship. I missed it too, and so we made plans to meet for breakfast." She reached for her glass and took another sip. "You know the rest of the story. She was killed before we even had a chance to find out if we could be friends again."

Vivian and Freddie exchanged glances. Vivian found herself moved by what she saw – a woman who'd lost both her husband and her best friend, and was doing what she could to repair the damage.

"I wanted to hate her for what she did," Neville said, "but then I found out that I wanted her friendship more." She gave a sad smile. "Pathetic, huh? Your best friend breaks up your marriage and you still can't let go." She looked up at Vivian and Freddie. "You sure you won't have a drink?"

FIFTY-EIGHT

FREDDIE LOOKED BACK AT NEVILLE'S CONDO AS HE CLIMBED ONTO Vivian's Triumph Bonneville. He could feel the engine rumbling beneath him. He imagined Neville pouring herself another round as the day closed in around her.

"So what do you think, love?" he said over the sound of the engine.

"I think it's a really sad story," Vivian said. "She lost everything and has to live with it."

"Quite, but did she do it?"

Vivian revved the engine. "I don't know. She could have." She turned to Freddie. "Where to?"

"Fancy a bite?"

An hour later Vivian pulled up in front of The Pig and Whistle, an English pub on Geary Boulevard in the Laurel District. She looked out at the pub.

"You want to go here?" she said.

"Indeed," Freddie said as he climbed off the bike. "Ever been here?"

Vivian shook her head. "Never heard of it."

"Well, then, you're in for a bit of a treat."

They went inside. Vivian stood in the doorway for a moment and looked around. A soccer game was in progress on the giant flat-screen

TV mounted above the bar. Fans wearing team jerseys were hoisting beer mugs and cheering their teams on. Others were playing darts and shouting orders at the bartenders.

"Looks like a full house," Freddie said, scanning the room for an empty table. "We'll sit at the bar."

They crawled onto two empty stools and some moments later the bartender, a redhead wearing a soccer team jersey, came up to them and dropped menus on the bar in front of them.

"What's it gonna be then?" the bartender said in an East End London accent.

"Newcastle Brown Ale," Freddie said.

The bartender looked at Vivian. "And for you, love?"

"I'll have the same," she said.

Freddie grinned. "Living it up, are we, love?"

"Easy then," the bartender said. "You want food too?"

Freddie nodded. "Give us a minute."

"Right," the bartender said, and moved away to make their drinks.

"What are you gonna have?" Vivian said, scanning the menu.

"Fish and chips," Freddie said. "You?"

"Do they have salads? I don't see any on the menu."

Freddie took on a pained expression. "Salads? In an English pub? They'll throw you out, love."

Vivian grinned. "Just kidding. I'll go for the fish and chips too."

Freddie looked relieved. "Now you're talking like a right proper Brit."

The bartender returned with their ales and Freddie placed their orders for fish and chips.

"Cheers then," Freddie said, hosting his mug.

"What are we drinking to?" Vivian said.

Freddie shrugged.

"The truth, love," he said as he sipped his ale. "What else?"

"You think we got the truth from Laura Neville?"

Freddie paused to think about it, then nodded. "It was too sad to be a lie."

"She still could've killed her."

"She said she didn't own a gun or know how to use one."

Vivian scoffed. "It's easy to get a gun, and then all you have to do is point and shoot."

"Yes, quite," Freddie said.

"If she did own a gun she would've had to register it, right?" Vivian said. "Maybe you could check and see if there's a record of her buying a gun."

Freddie looked at Vivian. "So you don't believe her?"

"Yeah, I do believe her. I'm just not sure about the part about the gun."

"Why?"

"You know what they say about a woman scorned. Maybe she wanted to make up with Joanna so she could get close enough to shoot her."

"That's a bit cold, isn't it?"

"Murder's a bit cold, Freddie."

Freddie nodded. He worked the crime beat long enough to know that nothing ran colder than cold-blooded murder. The bartender returned with their fish and chips and set the plates down in front of Freddie and Vivian.

"Lovely," Freddie said, beaming with expectation as he looked at his plate.

Vivian took a sip of her ale, then began eating. "Hey, this is really good."

Freddie smiled. "Better than a salad, then?"

They fell silent as they ate. Vivian could hear the sound of the game on TV and the shouts of the fans all around her cheering on their teams.

"What about Sylvia and Floyd Ritter?" she said breaking the silence.

"What about them?

"I feel like everybody's holding out on us."

"What do you mean?"

"Laura Neville held out on us about the affair and the blackmail, and Sylvia never told me about her affair with Ritter."

"Yes, well, that's the whole point of an affair, isn't it? It's supposed to be a secret. What about the chap that called you and tried to scare you off? Don't you suppose he's the killer?"

"Maybe. But maybe he wasn't working alone." Vivian sipped her ale and looked at Freddie.

Freddie chuckled and sipped his ale. "Right. Maybe all three of them – Laura, Sylvia and Floyd – got together and decided to kill Joanna Rorke."

"Very funny," Vivian said. "There's just one problem."

"What's that?"

"What's Floyd's motive? Joanna stole Ben's book, not his, right?"

"Come to think of it, what about that book?" Freddie said. "Bus driver by day, mystery writer by night?"

"Yeah, and why do all three books tell the same story? We still haven't figured that one yet."

"Good question," Freddie said. "But I reckon that finding the answer might get us killed."

"I wonder where the police are on the case," Vivian said, exchanging glances with Freddie. "It's not like we can ask them, right?"

"I can," Freddie said. "I'm a crime reporter, remember? I'll pop round tomorrow and see what I can find out." He raised his mug, which was nearly empty. "Fancy another round?"

Vivian gave a regretful smile. "Can't. I'm driving."

They called it a night after that. Vivian dropped Freddie off, then headed back across town. The sun was setting as she rode home, throwing shadows on the streets that reminded her of the secrets that lay hidden in the dark. There was still so much that she and Freddie didn't know, and as she pulled into the garage she wondered if they would ever learn the truth about Joanna's death.

She parked the bike and went up to her apartment. Then she unlocked the door and went inside.

"Close the door," Sylvia said, pointing a gun at Vivian.

FIFTY-NINE

VIVIAN STARED AT THE GUN, AND AT THE WOMAN HOLDING IT IN HER hand. Sylvia was sitting in one of the chairs facing the sofa. She was wearing sweats and a hoodie, and looked as if she'd been there awhile. A backpack rested on the floor beside her.

"What are doing here?" she said.

"Waiting for you."

"How'd you get into my apartment?"

"Never mind that," Sylvia said. She nodded at the sofa. "Sit down."

Vivian sat on the edge of the sofa across from Sylvia, her eyes riveted on the gun. Sylvia seemed nervous, jittery, and Vivian was terrified that at any moment the gun might go off.

"Where is it?" Sylvia said.

"Where's what?"

"Don't play dumb with me, sweetie. I know you have it because I gave it to you."

Then it hit Vivian. "The flash drive?"

"Where is it?"

"It was you that broke in last time, wasn't it?"

"Yeah, it was me. So what?"

"You gave me the wrong one, didn't you? You meant to give me *Tourist Trap* but you gave me something called *Death Trip*."

"I made a mistake."

"Why is it so important?"

"That's none of your business. Just give me the flash drive. I gotta go."

"It's in my purse," Vivian said, nodding at the cross-body bag slung over her shoulder.

"Hand it over."

"Sure, no problem," Vivian said.

She pulled the bag off her shoulder and began rummaging through it.

"Hurry up!" Sylvia said.

Just then there was a knock at the door. Vivian saw Sylvia take her eyes off her and glance at the door.

"Hey Viv, you home?" a woman said. "Want to hang out?"

Shondra, Vivian thought. Just what she needed. She swung the bag at Sylvia, who was distracted by the knock at the door, and knocked the gun out of her hand. It skated across the floor in Vivian's direction. Sylvia lunged for it, but Vivian grabbed it before she could reach it.

"You in there, Viv?" Shondra said.

Vivian put her fingers to her lips. She settled into a chair across from Sylvia and pointed the gun at her. She waited until she was certain Shondra had given up and gone back to her apartment. Then she looked at Sylvia and said, "Okay, let's talk. Just us girls."

Sylvia took on a sullen expression. "Why should I talk to you?"

Vivian shrugged. "Because I'm the one with the gun and the flash drive, remember?"

"You don't know what you've gotten yourself into," Sylvia said.

"You're right, I don't. So why don't you tell me about it?"

"I can't."

"Why not?"

"Because if I do I'm dead."

"I don't understand. What are you talking about?"

"I mean he'll kill me." Sylvia gave a cold smile. "Might kill you too."

"Who's he?"

Sylvia shook her head.

"Why's the flash drive so important? And why do all three books have the same story?"

"I already told you. Joanna stole Ben's book."

"Yeah, but you didn't tell me about *Death Trip*. I wasn't supposed to know about that, right?"

"I can't talk about that."

"You can't talk about anything, can you? You had plenty to say about Joanna, but that wasn't the whole story, was it?"

Sylvia looked sharply at Vivian. "You don't need to know the whole story. It's none of your business anyway. Just give me the drive and I'll be out of your life."

"Just like that, huh?" Vivian said.

"Yeah, just like that."

"It's not that simple and you know it."

"Yeah, why's that?"

"I know about you and Floyd Ritter."

The color drained out of Sylvia's face. She stared at Vivian. "How do you know about that?"

"I just know, okay? Did Ben know?"

Sylvia shook her head. "He never found out."

"Are you sure? Was that why he killed himself?"

Sylvia glared at Vivian. "You don't know what the hell you're talking about. Me and Floyd had nothing to do with it."

"Is it still going on, you and Floyd?"

Sylvia said nothing.

"You still haven't told me why the flash drive is so important."

"I don't want him to know I took it."

"Floyd?"

Sylvia nodded.

"Why'd you take it?"

Sylvia shook her head. "I can't tell you."

"Can't, or won't?"

"Take your pick. I still can't tell you."

"Sounds like you're afraid of him."

Sylvia looked up at Vivian and the fear in her eyes gave the answer.

"Please, just give me the drive, okay?"

"Why won't you tell me what's going on?"

Sylvia's eyes flashed with anger. "Because I don't want to end up like Joanna, okay? Is that good enough for you? Who the hell are you anyway, butting into something that doesn't concern you? You think because you spent the night with her you got a right to know?"

She was right, Vivian thought. She had no right to know, and yet she had to know. She reached into her purse and pulled out the flash drive and gave it to Sylvia.

"Thanks," Sylvia said with a grateful smile. She reached down and put the flash drive in her backpack.

Vivian nodded at the gun in her hand. "Were you gonna shoot me?"

Sylvia shook her head. "I just wanted to scare you."

"So I'd be as afraid as you are?" Vivian said.

"Maybe."

Vivian handed the gun to Sylvia. She shoved it in the backpack, then stood and looked at Vivian.

"Don't get in any deeper," she said. "You may not be able to climb back out." Sylvia pushed past Vivian and walked out of her apartment.

Vivian tried to calm down. No one had ever pointed a gun at her before.

Then she heard the gunshots.

She rushed out of her apartment and went down the stairs to the front door. She ran outside and then stopped cold. Sylvia was lying dead on the sidewalk in front of her building in a spreading pool of blood.

Ever want to kill somebody? Me too! That's why I love Murder Tours.

NAME WITHHELD

SIXTY

Vivian sat in a chair while Bassett and Chen paced back and forth in front of her. *At least I'm not trapped in some windowless police interrogation room,* she thought. Then it occurred to her that she had chosen to sit in the same chair that Sylvia sat in just before she was gunned down in front of her building. Still, she didn't move.

"So… here we are again, Ms. Voss," Bassett said. "You just can't seem to mind your own business, can you?"

Vivian looked up sharply at Bassett. "She broke into my apartment, okay? It wasn't like I invited her. By the way, did you talk to her?"

"Yeah, we talked to her," Bassett said. "She had an alibi for the time Joanna Rorke was killed."

"Okay, let's take it from the top," Chen said. "You said Sylvia Torrey was in your apartment when you got home, and that she was armed."

Vivian nodded. "I don't know how she got in."

"You said she wanted a flash drive she had given you."

Vivian nodded.

"What was so important about the flash drive?"

"There was a manuscript on it, a mystery called *Death Trip*."

"Who wrote it?"

"The bus driver."

Bassett and Chen exchanged glances.

"Excuse me?" Bassett said.

"His name's Floyd Ritter. He drives the *Murder Tours* bus."

"How'd you end up with it?"

"Sylvia gave it to me."

Why?"

"She meant to give me a flash drive with her husband's book on it—"

"*Tourist Trap?*" Bassett said.

Vivian nodded. "But instead it had Ritter's book on it. I think she was afraid he was gonna find out she took it."

"Why did it matter?"

"I don't know, but it did."

Bassett took on an incredulous expression. "Sylvia Torrey was killed over a book?"

"I don't know, but they were involved."

"Sylvia and Floyd?"

Vivian nodded. "Did she tell you about him?"

"No."

"What did she tell you about the books?"

"She told us about how Rorke allegedly plagiarized her husband Ben's book. You're saying there's a third book?"

Vivian nodded. "Ritter's book. *Death Trip*. And the story's the same as the other two books."

"Three different books with the same story?"

Vivian nodded. "Did you talk to Ritter?"

"No, we had no reason to."

"Well, maybe you do now."

"Why's that?"

"Because they knew each other, Floyd and Sylvia and her husband. They went on a tour with Floyd before Ben died. So he must know something about it."

"Ben Torrey's death was ruled a suicide," Bassett said.

"Yeah, I know. That's what Sylvia told me. But now she's dead too."

"So if all three books are the same, who stole from whom?"

"I don't know. Sylvia wouldn't tell me."

"I don't get it," Chen said.

"I don't either," Vivian said, "but I'm scared." She looked up at Bassett and Chen. "What if I'm next?"

"Why's the killer gonna come after you? Did you write a book too?" Bassett said.

"He called me," Vivian said.

"Who called you?"

"The man who killed Joanna Rorke."

"How do you know he was the killer?"

"It had to be him. He had my number."

"How'd he get it?" Chen said.

"I jotted it down on a notepad when I was with Joanna. He must've found it."

"What did he say?"

"He said he knew I was there and he told me to forget what I saw or the same thing would happen to me."

"That was it?" Chen said.

Vivian nodded.

"You got yourself in deep, didn't you, girl?" Bassett said.

Vivian looked up at her. "Yeah, I guess I did," she said.

"You got someplace to go now that he knows where you live?"

SIXTY-ONE

THE LIGHT CHANGED. VIVIAN TWISTED THE THROTTLE AND THE BIKE shot through an empty intersection. It was late and traffic was light, and all she wanted to do was put miles between herself and Sylvia's body lying dead in the street outside her building. It occurred to her that she was the last person to see Sylvia before she was murdered. Just like she was the last person to see Joanna alive before she was killed. *Am I some sort of angel of death,* Vivian wondered, *or does it just mean that I'm next?* She followed the double yellow line unspooling in front of her. Soon she would be there. Soon she would be safe.

Then she noticed the car behind her. It was coming up fast, getting closer and closer. The headlights were on high beam, lighting up the street in front of her and blinding her when she glanced in her mirrors. Vivian could hear the thrash of heavy metal over the sound of the bike and assumed that the driver had the windows down. She accelerated to put distance between herself and the car, but as she did so the driver sped up to keep pace with her. She changed lanes and the driver changed with her. Block after block he stayed with her, as if to remind her that he was still there.

Vivian could feel herself starting to sweat. *Who is it?* she wondered. *Why is he following me? Is it him? Is he coming after me now?* Then the car got closer. Close enough to give her a tap that would send her flying head-first over the handlebars. The music seemed to get even louder, electric guitars shredding the night air. Vivian tried to get a glimpse of the driver in her mirrors, but all she saw were headlights. The driver began flashing his lights at her, as if to disorient her and throw her off her game.

Vivian twisted the throttle, riding faster and faster, the streets flashing past her as she raced to outrun the car. But she knew that if she went any faster she would lose control. She had to lose him before he slammed into her. Then the driver pulled out alongside her. Vivian glanced at the driver but saw nothing. The sound of the music was deafening. *He's going to sideswipe me,* Vivian thought. *Total the bike and me along with it.* The driver veered toward her. The bike's tires squealed as Vivian swerved to avoid him. Her overnight bag flew off her shoulder and landed in the street. No way she could stop to retrieve it.

Then the driver turned in again. But this time, instead of swerving to avoid him, Vivian jumped the curb and raced down the sidewalk. The driver tried to follow her, but the cars parked nose to tail along the street made it impossible for him. Up ahead, a strip mall. Vivian saw a narrow pedestrian alley between two shops. She braked hard, throwing the bike into a skid, then turned down the alley and killed the light. She heard the screech of brakes as the driver tried to follow her. But she was gone. She rode in the dark until she was sure she had lost him, then pulled over and turned off the engine. She was sweating and her heart was pounding. Someone had tried to kill her. He would try again. She sat in the dark until she could breathe.

SIXTY-TWO

"Who is it?" Freddie said.

"It's me," Vivian said, breathing hard.

It was two in the morning and she was standing in the hallway outside Freddie's apartment. She was slick with sweat and an adrenaline rush was racing through her body like an electric current.

The door opened. Freddie peered out at Vivian, surprised to see her. He was wearing a bathrobe and looked as if he had just woken up.

"Hello, love," he said. He rubbed his eyes. "What are you doing here?"

"He tried to kill me," she said. Her eyes darted around the hallway, as if afraid that he had somehow followed her into the building and was coming up the stairs after her. Then she pushed past Freddie and went inside and slammed the door.

"What are you saying? Who tried to kill you," Freddie said, waking up fast.

"She's dead and he tried to kill me too. Tried to run me off the road."

Then Vivian heard Barbara call out from the bedroom. "Who is it, love?"

Vivian glanced toward the bedroom and suddenly felt awkward. "I guess this isn't a good time, huh?"

"Never mind that. Who's dead?"

"Sylvia."

Freddie stared at her. "What?"

"He shot her in front of my building. And now he's after me." She looked at Freddie. "He knows where I live."

Just then Barbara came out of the bedroom, also wearing a bathrobe.

"Hi…" she said, surprised to see Vivian. Then she saw the fear on Vivian's face. "What's happened?"

"A woman's been murdered," Freddie said.

Barbara gasped. "Murdered! How awful."

"Sit down, love," Freddie said, "tell me what happened."

Vivian sank into the sofa. Freddie sat down next to her.

"She was in my apartment when you dropped me off."

"Sylvia?"

Vivian nodded. "I don't know how she got in. But she had a gun and she told me to give her the flash drive."

"Did you?"

Vivian nodded. "I tried to find out what she knew but she wouldn't tell me anything. Then after she left I heard gunshots and when I went downstairs, she was dead." Vivian buried her face in her hands. Then she looked up at Freddie and Barbara. "I'm sorry for showing up in the middle of the night like this…"

"It's okay, love."

"Not to worry," Barbara said, "you're safe with us."

"And then when I was riding over here I noticed a car following me…" Vivian ran her hands through her hair. "He tried to run me off the road and kill me. I dropped my overnight bag with Floyd and Sylvia's emails in it and I couldn't go back and get it."

"Who tried to run you off the road?"

"I don't know, but it has to be the same person who killed Sylvia, and maybe killed Joanna too." She looked at Freddie. "Can I stay here? He knows where I live."

"You can stay here as long as you like," Freddie said.

Vivian looked at Barbara. "I don't want to be in the way or anything…"

"You mean me and Freddie? You won't be in the way unless you jump in bed with us."

Vivian smiled in spite of her fear. Freddie turned to Nigel and Claire, who were curled up in an overstuffed chair. "Me lovelies won't mind either."

Vivian gave a grateful smile. "Thanks."

"Fancy a cuppa tea?"

"Yeah, that sounds great," Vivian said.

"I'll just go and put the kettle on."

Freddie stood and went into the kitchen. Barbara sat down next to Vivian.

"You poor thing. First a woman's murdered and then someone tries to kill you."

Vivian nodded, then turned to Barbara. "I'm sorry, I didn't know you were here."

"It's fine, love. I'll be out of your hair in the morning. I've got a flight back to London."

"Oh no, please, I didn't mean it like that…I'm glad you're here and I know Freddie's glad you're here."

Barbara smiled. "Not to worry, I'll be back. Now that the old boy and I have reconnected, I don't want to lose touch again."

"Good, glad to hear it," Vivian said.

Freddie walked back into the living room with a tray containing a tea kettle and three teacups and set it down on the coffee table.

"The cops showed up afterwards, the same ones we talked to before," Vivian said.

"Bassett and Chen?"

"Yeah. They told me they talked to Sylvia and she had an alibi for when Joanna was murdered. But now she's dead too. I'm scared, Freddie. He's after me too."

"I doubt he'll look for you here," Freddie said. He poured two cups of tea and handed them to Vivian and Barbara. Vivian wrapped her hands around the teacup as if its warmth could console her.

She sipped her tea, then turned to Freddie. "The cops didn't know about Floyd. I told them what I knew, which wasn't much."

Freddie nodded. "I reckon they'll follow up with Floyd now that they know about him."

"What are we supposed to do in the meantime?"

"Let the coppers do their job. You need to lay low now, love."

"I'm not gonna let him scare me off," Vivian said defiantly, as if bravado could overcome her fear.

Freddie gave a gentle smile. "You wouldn't be here if you weren't scared."

Vivian paused. Had she come this far for nothing? She looked down into her teacup, then turned to Freddie. "So that's it? We're done? You want to give up?"

"Nobody said anything about giving up, but you've been through a bit of an ordeal tonight, and you should get some rest. We'll talk in the morning."

Vivian shook her head. "I'll rest when I know who killed Joanna and why. I think Sylvia knew the truth and maybe that's why she's dead."

"Yes, well, we don't want you to be next, do we, love?"

SIXTY-THREE

BEING NEXT WAS ALL VIVIAN COULD THINK OF AS SHE TRIED TO SLEEP. She was afraid the first time she slept in Freddie's bed, and she was afraid again now. *He doesn't know where I am,* she told herself. *He can't find me here.* And yet, as she tossed and turned in a ragged sleep, she could not shake the feeling that there was nowhere to hide. She was racing through the night on a used Triumph Bonneville, and the car behind her was getting closer and closer.

The next morning, relieved to discover that she was still alive, Vivian borrowed Freddie's Jag, which was back on the road again after being towed to his mechanic for repairs.

"My mechanic told me he was glad I drove a British car," Freddie said with a rueful smile as he handed over the keys, "because the bills paid for his son's college tuition."

In her rush to escape her apartment after Sylvia was killed, Vivian had only brought what she could carry on her motorcycle. She didn't know how long she'd hide out at Freddie's place, but she was going to need more than an overnight change of clothes.

Freddie had told her he'd be happy to do it for her, but she told him she felt safe enough in the light of day to do it herself. But as she packed a bag in her apartment, Vivian felt as if she had returned to the

227

scene of the crime. Sylvia wasn't killed inside her apartment, but she was gunned down the moment she walked out of the building, which made it seem way too close for comfort.

Still, being afraid to stay in her apartment made Vivian feel as if she was homeless. *Will I ever be able to return?* she wondered. *Or will I have to move to another apartment and try to forget what happened? It was all my fault,* she thought. *Why did I have to take it upon myself to learn the truth about Joanna's death? Was it because I slept with her? Was that enough reason?*

Maybe Freddie was right, she thought. Maybe the time had come to stop playing detective, especially now that someone had tried to kill her. Was the satisfaction of knowing who killed Joanna worth her life? And what if she did find out who killed her? Joanna would still be dead, and the fact that her killer had been brought to justice would bring her no satisfaction. *Only the living could be satisfied,* Vivian thought. *The dead were out of luck.*

Then her intercom buzzed, interrupting the thoughts tumbling through her mind. Vivian glanced at the intercom as her stomach tightened and the fear rose in her throat. *Was it him?* she thought, politely asking to be buzzed in so he could kill her? She walked over to the intercom and pressed the button.

"Yes?"

"Hi Vivian, it's Ethan." He paused, then said, "Ethan Rorke."

"Hi," Vivian said, taken by surprise.

"I'm on my way to the airport. Just wanted to say goodbye. Can I come up?"

"Sure," Vivian said, and buzzed him into the building.

Moments later the doorbell rang. Vivian walked over to the door and opened it.

Ethan gave a tight smile. "Hi."

"Hi, come in," Vivian said.

"Thanks," Ethan said, and walked into the apartment.

"I didn't expect to see you again," Vivian said as she closed the door.

"Going somewhere?" Ethan said, nodding at the overnight bag.

"Yeah, I'm housesitting for a couple of days," Vivian lied. She nodded at the sofa. "Have a seat. You want anything? I think I might have some wine left."

"I'm good, thanks," Ethan said.

"So you're leaving, huh?"

"Yeah, the police released my Mom's body, so I'm taking her back home." Ethan paused, then looked at Vivian. "They told me," he said quietly.

"They told you what?" Vivian said, feeling a sudden, nameless dread.

"About you and my Mom."

Vivian gasped, as if the wind had been knocked out of her. She felt the heat rush into her face as she sank into a chair. He knew.

"How did you find out?" she said, looking down at her hands.

"The cops let it slip. I guess it was too juicy to keep it a secret."

"I'm sorry," Vivian said. "I never wanted you to know."

"Yeah, no shit. Is that why you didn't want to see me again?"

Vivian forced herself to look up at Ethan. "I was afraid you'd find out and then we'd have to talk about it and it would be really weird."

"Yeah, and then I found out anyway."

Vivian nodded. They fell silent. She wished more than anything that she could just disappear, anything rather than have to talk to Ethan about how she had sex with his mother.

"Are you pissed at me or what?" Vivian said.

Ethan gave a shrug. "To tell you the truth, I don't know how I feel. Never went through something like this before."

"Yeah, well, that makes two of us."

"You mind telling me how it happened?"

"It just happened, okay? I went to her reading, we had a couple drinks and one thing led to another."

"Is that what usually happens when you go to readings? You hook up with the author?"

Vivian looked sharply at Ethan, her eyes flashing with anger. "No, it's not what usually happens when I go to a reading. The author getting murdered afterwards is also not what usually happens."

She saw Ethan flinch, and immediately regretted having said it. "Sorry," she said quietly. "I shouldn't have said that."

"I should go," Ethan said, and stood.

Vivian stood and looked at him. "I'm sorry," she said. "I wish none of it had happened."

Ethan nodded. "Yeah, me too." Then he walked to the door and opened it.

"Can I ask you something?" Vivian said.

Ethan turned to her and waited.

"Was that the only reason you wanted to see me?"

Ethan smiled sadly and shook his head. "No, but it's the one reason I wish I could forget." Then he walked out, closing the door behind him.

Vivian took a deep breath, then let it out slowly. She glanced at the door. Ethan would be walking to the elevator, or maybe taking the stairs. She could go after him and tell him that perhaps in time things could be different. Not everything between them had to be about what happened with Joanna. It was a shock now, but eventually it would fade into the past like everything else. All they had to do was give it a chance.

But Vivian knew better. It would never fade into the past and Ethan would never get over it. Joanna would be always be with them, like some threesome from the grave. She finished packing her bag, then headed out the door.

SIXTY-FOUR

FREDDIE NOSED THE JAG INTO THE CURB IN FRONT OF THE International Terminal at SFO, then turned to Barbara, who was sitting beside him.

"Well, here we are love. Not too late to change your mind, you know."

Barbara smiled, then leaned across the seat and kissed him.

"Come on, love, we'd best get my bags out of the boot."

Freddie and Barbara got out of the car under the watchful eye of an airport traffic cop, whose job it was to make sure no one lingered longer than it took to say goodbye. Freddie opened the trunk and took out Barbara's luggage. He set the bags on the sidewalk and pulled up the handles so she could wheel them into the terminal. Then it was time to say goodbye.

They embraced, then Barbara pulled back and looked at Freddie. "Take care of yourself. And take care of Vivian too. It's all quite exciting what you're doing, but I don't want anything to happen to either one of you." She paused, then said, "I want you here when I get back."

Freddie smiled. "Come back soon, love."

Barbara smiled and seemed to tear up. "I promise."

Then she turned and went into the terminal. Freddie watched her until she was gone, then got back in the car and pulled away from those who were leaving and those, like him, who were left behind. As he merged into traffic, Freddie realized that he suddenly missed Barbara more than he had in the years since he left London for another life in the States. And he hoped that seeing each other again had meant as much to her as it did to him.

He jumped on 101 North and headed back to the city. The SFPD was holding a press conference on the Joanna Rorke case, and Freddie didn't want to be late.

———

THE PRESS CONFERENCE was held in a meeting room on the fifth floor of SFPD headquarters on Bryant Street. Freddie arrived a few minutes before 11am.

"Hey Freddie," a young Asian woman said as he walked into the room. "How do you figure they're gonna spin it?"

Freddie smiled. Her name was Kim and she covered the SFPD for the *San Jose Mercury News*. "Search me," he said. "I reckon we're about to find out."

He glanced toward the front of the room. Detectives Bassett and Chen had stepped to the podium and appeared to be reviewing their notes prior to the start of the press conference. Freddie remembered that he had met them the night he and Vivian and Barbara had gone to Buddha Lounge to interview Kyle Crosby. But instead of getting answers to their questions about Crosby's connection to Joanna Rorke, they wound up in a brawl outside the bar when Crosby assaulted Barbara. Now Freddie wondered if Bassett and Chen would remember him.

"What are you hearing?" Kim said.

That was Kim, Freddie thought. *Always probing for the story, even if it meant stealing a scoop from a fellow reporter.*

"Same as you, I reckon," Freddie said.

Kim gave a sly smile, then pursued another line of inquiry. "How are things over at the *Sentinel?*" she said. "I hear layoffs are coming. You worried?"

"Ladies and gentlemen, if I could have your attention, please," Chen said. "We're about ready to start. I'll take the first question."

"We'd better take our seats," Freddie said, ignoring Kim's probe about layoffs. He smiled politely, then moved away from her and settled into an aisle seat.

A grizzled, old-school reporter in the front row raised his hand. Freddie knew him well. His name was Cal and he and Freddie had worked together at the *Sentinel* before Cal moved to the *Chronicle*. Cal had been married and divorced three times, each time to a bartender. He liked to drink and thought it might be a good idea if he kept it in the family. It didn't work out that way, but Freddie figured Cal would keep trying until he got it right, or his liver gave out.

"Yes, Cal," the detective said.

"What's the latest on the Joanna Rorke case? What can you share with us?"

"The homicide investigation is proceeding," Chen replied. "We're continuing to gather evidence."

"What kind of evidence?" Cal said.

"You know better than that, Cal," Bassett said. "When the time comes we'll be happy to share what we have with the media."

Reporters' hands shot up, including Freddie's. Chen looked out at the reporters, then pointed at Freddie.

"Yes?"

"Freddie Fraser, *San Francisco Sentinel.*"

"What's your question?"

"Do you have any suspects in the case?"

"We've identified several persons of interest, and we're following up with them."

Freddie followed up. "Is Kyle Crosby one of them? Does he have an alibi?"

Chen's face tightened. *Now he remembers me*, Freddie thought. "No comment," Chen said.

"What about Floyd Ritter?" Freddie said.

Chen ignored him. He pointed at another reporter. "Yes?"

"Who are Kyle Crosby and Floyd Ritter?" the reporter asked.

Bassett and Chen exchanged glances, then glared at Freddie, who had opened up a new line of questioning.

"As we said, we've identified persons of interest, but we're not identifying anyone at this time," Chen said.

"Are you worried about the case going cold?" a reporter asked. "You know what they say about the first 48 hours."

"Yeah, we know what they say," Bassett said. "But here's what we say: No way is this case is gonna go cold, okay?"

"Okay, one more question," Chen said. "He pointed at a reporter. "Yes?"

"Does the fact that Joanna Rorke was a bestselling author instead of a Tenderloin junkie put greater pressure on the department to solve the case?"

"We put ourselves under pressure to solve every homicide, no matter who the victim was." Bassett said. She looked out at the reporters. "Thanks for coming."

Reporters shouted out questions as Bassett and Chen moved away from the podium, but they appeared to fall on deaf ears. Freddie stood and prepared to leave. Kim rushed over to him.

"Who's Kyle Crosby?"

Freddie smiled. "No comment."

"C'mon, Freddie, give a girl a break."

"Lovely to see you again, Kim," Freddie said, and headed for the door.

"Hey! *San Francisco Sentinel!*" a woman shouted.

Freddie turned and saw Bassett and Chen coming toward him. They didn't look happy.

"What the hell were you doing back there?" Bassett said, her face twisted with anger.

"My job," Freddie replied.

"Your job, huh? Since when is hijacking SFPD press conferences your job?"

"I wasn't hijacking anything; I was simply asking a question. You chose not to answer it. Will you answer it now? And while we're on the subject, who else is a person of interest?"

"I'm warning you, Fraser. You keep asking the wrong questions I'll see to it that your press credentials are revoked."

"My apologies," Freddie said. "I didn't realize that there were right and wrong questions."

Bassett gave Freddie a long hard stare, and as she did so her face lit up with recognition.

"Hey, wait a minute. I know why you were asking about Kyle Crosby. You were involved in that fight with Crosby at Buddha Lounge. You and the girl—"

"Vivian Voss," Freddie said.

"Yeah, that's her," Chen said.

"And you are?"

"Freddie Fraser, at your service."

"Right. Freddie Fraser. You're quite the pair, you and the girl, aren't you?" Bassett said.

Freddie said nothing.

"What do you know about Floyd Ritter?"

"I was hoping you would tell me."

"What's that supposed to mean?"

"He's a person of interest, isn't he?"

"Maybe, maybe not," Bassett said. "But your girlfriend told us about him too. She still playing detective?"

"She better not be," Chen said. "I'd hate to have to haul her ass in." He looked at Freddie. "Maybe yours, too."

"Is that a threat?" Freddie said.

Bassett and Chen exchanged glances.

"Not at all," Chen said with a mocking smirk. "We're here to serve and protect, remember?"

"It's just a friendly suggestion," Bassett said. Then she smiled. "You want to stay on our good side, don't you?"

Bassett and Chen turned and walked away from him. *That went well*, Freddie thought. Then his cell phone rang.

"You got a vacuum cleaner?" Vivian said.

SIXTY-FIVE

VIVIAN STOOD IN THE LIVING ROOM, ONE HAND ON FREDDIE'S AGED vacuum cleaner, and surveyed the task at hand. There was no sign of Nigel or Claire, who had vanished once they saw the vacuum cleaner. The room was a shambles, but that was nothing new. It was just Freddie. The disarray was his décor. The sofa, which looked as if he'd found it at a Goodwill store, was covered with fur balls and sagging under the weight of years of use. Empty bottles and cans, clothes, old magazines and newspapers, and ashtrays filled to overflowing littered the room. She walked into the kitchen and surveyed the damage. Empty pizza boxes and takeout cartons were stacked on the counter and the sink was filled with dirty dishes, cups and glasses. The bedroom was no better. The bed was unmade, there were dirty glasses on the nightstands and dirty clothes were in a jumble on the floor.

Where to begin? Vivian asked herself. *And what would Freddie think of her decision to take it upon herself to mess with his environment? It didn't matter what he thought,* Vivian concluded. If she was going to stay with him, things had to change. She couldn't live with Freddie's disarray. Whether he could live with her neatness remained to be seen. But there was more to it than that. Vivian knew that she needed to stay busy to keep the fear at bay. Otherwise it would consume her.

She walked back into the living and switched on the vacuum cleaner. It wheezed into life and Vivian began pushing it across the carpet. When she was finished with the carpets she vacuumed the fur balls on the sofa. Loose change rattled through the tube when she vacuumed between the cushions. She had to change the bag twice before she was done. She put the vacuum away, then emptied the ashtrays and dusted the furniture. She glanced at Freddie's desk, which was covered with papers and documents, but decided against making any changes, as it was Freddie's workspace, and thus off limits.

Finished with the living room, she tackled the kitchen. She dumped the pizza boxes and takeout cartons in the trash cans behind the building, then washed and dried the dishes and put them away. Then she went into the bathroom. She paused as she scanned the toilet, sink and shower. Vivian never minded cleaning her own bathroom, but cleaning someone else's bathroom, especially one as messy as this one, made her feel like a maid. Still, it had to be done, if only because using it in its current state was even worse.

When she was finished she went into the bedroom. She made the bed and sorted the clothes that were in a pile on the floor. She was in the process of clearing the nightstands when she found a photo album. She sat on the bed and opened the album and began leafing through it.

There were photographs of Freddie's family and of Freddie as a child. Vivian smiled to herself as she looked at photos of Freddie in his schoolboy uniform, standing with adults whom Vivian assumed were his parents. There also photos taken years ago of Freddie and Barbara in London. They were in each other's arms, smiling at the camera, the happiest couple in the world. The album transfixed Vivian, and for the moment she forgot all about cleaning the apartment, and simply looked through the window into Freddie's life.

"We were quite the dashing couple, eh?"

Vivian looked up, startled. Freddie stood in the doorway. She froze. Felt the blood rush into her face.

"I'm sorry…I was just cleaning up and I found it," Vivian said, mortified.

"That's quite all right," Freddie said. "I like to have a look myself sometimes."

"I love the ones of you and Barbara, you look so happy."

A sad smile softened Freddie's face. "Yes, we were." He looked around. "I must say, I wasn't sure I was in the right apartment when I came in. What the devil happened here?"

"I just kind of straightened things up. I hope you don't mind."

"No, I don't mind. It's all quite tidy, isn't it? But you probably terrified Nigel and Claire."

Vivian nodded. "They took off when they saw the vacuum." She closed the photo album and changed the subject. "Any news at the press conference?"

"No, not really. They're playing it quite close to the vest. But they didn't like me asking about Kyle Crosby or Floyd Ritter."

Vivian paused to take it in, then said, "Joanna's son showed up when I was in my apartment."

Freddie looked at her. "Ethan?"

Vivian nodded.

"What'd he want?"

"He knows about me and Joanna. The police told him."

Freddie took on a shocked expression. "Bloody hell. That must've been awkward."

"Yeah, it was, for both of us. I tried to explain what happened, but how can you tell somebody you slept with his mother?"

"Not easily, I reckon," Freddie said.

"Funny thing is, I kind of liked him, you know what I mean?"

Freddie gave an understanding smile. "Next time you meet a bloke you like, don't sleep with his mother."

Vivian threw him a rueful nod. "Yeah, especially if his mother gets murdered."

Vivian and Freddie exchanged glances; then, as if not knowing what else to say, fell silent.

SIXTY-SIX

Floyd Ritter parks the *Murder Tours* bus across the street from the building where she was killed.

One of the passengers, a young man wearing khaki cargo shorts and a Fisherman's Wharf T-shirt, pipes up. "Why are we stopping here, Floyd?"

"It's not on the tour," a white-haired grandmother offers.

"It might be one of these days," Ritter says.

"Why's that, Floyd?" asks a young boy who's on the bus with his parents.

Ritter points at the building. "Somebody was killed there. Right in front of the building. See the blood on the sidewalk?"

The passengers whip out their smartphones and start snapping pics.

"Who was killed," the grandmother asks.

"Her name was Sylvia Torrey," Ritter says. "You never heard of her."

"Can we get off the bus so we can get a closer look?"

"Sure, go right ahead," Ritter says.

He opens the door and the passengers scramble off the bus. He watches them out the window. They're standing in a cluster by the bus holding their smartphones high above their heads. *They can take all the pics they want,* he thinks, *but they don't know what they're looking at.* Blood in the street. What does that tell them about her? Nothing. He doesn't need smartphone pics to see her. He remembers her clearly. He remembers her husband, Ben, too. He remembers them all together, the three of them on the tour. He remembers how they came back for another tour. They were friends, weren't they? Didn't they wish him luck with the book? Now they're both dead. Ritter imagines that as well. Is it because he drives the murder bus that everyone around him is dying? Ritter has no idea. He makes a living out of murder and doesn't ask questions. He knew Sylvia and now he doesn't. Even though she shared his bed. But things were different then. What they knew about each other was different. *Perhaps that kept her alive,* Ritter thinks, *until it was too late.*

Time to go. Ritter honks the horn.

SIXTY-SEVEN

"I THINK WE SHOULD DO THE TOUR AGAIN," VIVIAN SAID. SHE WAS sitting on the sofa with her MacBook on her lap. The *Murder Tours* website was on the screen.

"Say what?" Freddie called out from the kitchen, where he was feeding Nigel and Claire.

"We should do the tour again," Vivian said, a little louder this time.

Freddie walked into the living room with a can of cat food and a spoon in his hands. "Do the tour again? Play bloody tourist again?"

Vivian nodded. "Remember what we saw last time?"

"You mean Joanna's book with the Hyatt Regency bookmark?"

Vivian nodded. "It was stuffed under his seat. That had to mean something, Freddie."

Freddie was unconvinced. "It means he bought the bloody book. It's a bestseller, remember? You're reading too much into it, love."

Vivian shook her head. "I don't think so. I want to get another look at Floyd Ritter and the tour is a perfect way to do it. We'll be on the bus with him. Maybe we'll see something we missed the first time around."

She'd seen Floyd Ritter before, of course, when she rode the bus to Joanna's reading at Coit Tower, and later when he drove past her building one afternoon. Plus, they'd already taken the tour once. Which, as far as Freddie was concerned, was more than enough. But so much had happened since then. And most of it had to do with murder. But there was more than just murder; there was also betrayal. Thanks to the emails they discovered when they broke into Ritter's office, Vivian and Freddie had learned that he was having an affair with Sylvia Torrey. Now she was dead too, along with her husband Ben and Joanna Rorke. What else was there to learn about Floyd Ritter?

Freddie shook his head wearily. "A crime reporter on a bloody murder tour. Not once, but twice. I hope my editor doesn't find out. I'd never live it down."

Vivian smiled. "Come on, you can stand it for an hour or two."

"Yes, I suppose so, but what's the point?"

Vivian shrugged. "I don't know. Maybe we'll find out he's the killer."

Freddie looked at her. "Find out he's the killer? You think he's going to jolly well announce it over the loudspeaker?"

Vivian smiled. "Come on, I want to get another look at him. And you might get a scoop."

"All right, then, no harm, I suppose."

Most of the tours were sold out – murder was popular, just so long as you weren't the one being murdered – but Vivian was able to score two tickets for the last tour of the day, which began at 5pm. Vivian didn't want to leave her bike in the parking lot and Freddie's Jag was still in the shop, so they took an Uber to the *Murder Tours* offices south of Market.

"Well, here we are again," Freddie said, looking out the window as the driver pulled up in front of the building.

"Weird, huh," Vivian said.

"Quite."

Freddie stubbed out his cigarette in the Uber's ashtray and paid the driver, then they stepped out of the car. Vivian looked around.

"There he is," she said, pointing to Ritter, who was standing by the door of a *Murder Tours* bus, punching tickets as tourists boarded the bus. A line snaked across the parking lot.

"Looks a bit grim tonight, doesn't he?" Freddie said.

"Murder'll do that to you, I guess," Vivian said. C'mon, let's get in line."

Vivian and Freddie took their places at the end of the line and slowly shuffled toward the bus with the rest of the tourists. When they reached the front of the line Vivian handed Ritter their tickets.

"Back again, huh?" Ritter said.

"You remember us?" Vivian said. She threw a surprised glance at Freddie, then looked at Ritter.

Ritter gave a grim smile. "Sure I do. I never forget a face when it comes to murder."

Vivian felt a chill run through her. And was it her imagination, or did he linger when he looked at her? The way he lingered when he drove past her house? Was that why she suddenly felt trapped as she and Freddie took the last two seats in the back of the bus and the doors hissed shut as Ritter pulled out of the lot?

SIXTY-EIGHT

FREDDIE CHECKED HIS MESSAGES ON HIS iPHONE. THERE WAS A TEXT from Tom asking for status on the Joanna Rorke story. Freddie replied that he was en route to interview a person of interest in the case. It wasn't true, of course; Floyd Ritter was a person of interest to Freddie and Vivian, but the SFPD had not confirmed that he was under investigation. And even if he was, Freddie wasn't on his way to interview him. He was simply along for the ride with Vivian and the rest of the tourists. Would it lead to more than a tour of crime scenes? Freddie had no idea. But it put them on the bus with Ritter, the closest they'd been to him since Joanna was murdered. Whether he turned out to be anything more than a bus driver and aspiring mystery writer remained to be seen.

Freddie slid the phone into his pocket, then glanced at the illustrated *Murder Tours* flyer that Ritter had handed out as everyone boarded the bus. It teased in lurid detail the crimes committed at each of the stops on the tour, as if to whet the tourists' appetites for the blood and gore that lay in store for them.

They could shudder as they learned that the Zebra Killers were part of a militant Black Muslim cult that was on the hunt for white children, because killing them was the quickest way to becoming a Death Angel.

Swear never to go hiking as they read that the Trailside Killer, who got his start torturing animals, murdered as many as ten people on the trails in Marin, Santa Cruz and San Francisco counties.

Avoid taking cabs when they discovered that the Zodiac Killer had shot a cab driver, then tore off pieces of his bloody shirt and sent them to local newspapers.

Never sit for a portrait, because The Doodler liked to sketch his victims before he stabbed them to death.

Freddie grinned at Vivian as he waved the flyer in Vivian's face. "Bit of a homicide hit parade, isn't it?"

She gave a tense smile. "Same as last time. I guess he hasn't gotten around to adding new stops to the tour."

"You mean murders, don't you?" Freddie said.

Vivian looked at him. Her face was tense. "Yeah, all the people killing each other in San Francisco aren't famous enough for a tour."

"You okay, love?" Freddie said.

Vivian nodded. "Yeah, just nervous, I guess."

"Because of Ritter?"

"I feel like he knows about us. Or maybe he knows about me."

"The bloke behind the wheel?"

Vivian nodded.

"How the devil would he know? The security guard couldn't identify you."

Vivian shrugged. "I don't know, forget it. Maybe this wasn't such a good idea."

What did she expect to learn? Freddie wondered. That murder could entertain the living? She seemed tense, as if she was waiting for something to happen, something she dreaded. As the bus rolled towards the first stop, which, according to the flyer, was the Chinatown restaurant that back in 1977 was the site of the Golden Dragon Massacre, Freddie thought about all the murders he'd covered in his years on the beat. It occurred to him that he could conduct his own murder tours, but they would be filled with killers and victims who would remain as anonymous in death as they were in life.

Freddie looked out the window as the bus rolled through Chinatown. It felt strange to be a spectator at the scene of the crime, instead of the reporter who covered the greed, rage, envy, jealousy, lust and hatred that drove people to inflict such grievous harm on each other.

"Did you cover any of these cases?" Vivian said, glancing at the flyer.

Freddie shook his head. "Before my time, love."

"I bet you covered plenty of murders though, huh?"

Freddie nodded. "Thirty years' worth of bloody mayhem. But none of 'em were famous enough to end up on a tour."

"Until Joanna, right?" Vivian said. "She's special, isn't she?"

Freddie looked at Vivian. "Yes, quite special," he said. "She's the first one I've covered that might turn us into victims too."

The bus rolled on, one notorious crime scene after another. The Golden Dragon Massacre was followed by the Zodiac Killer, who then gave way to the Zebra Killers. Then came The Trailside Killer and Richard Ramirez, The Night Stalker. Freddie had thought of the tour as a homicide hit parade, but it could have just as easily been a homicide Hall of Fame. All the greats were here, drenched in blood and worth the price of a ticket.

He listened as Ritter kept up a running commentary on the killings that was filled with lurid details about each of the cases. As the passengers followed along and snapped smartphone pics, Freddie wondered if Ritter ever got sick of saying the same thing over and over again, and driving the same route day after day. But then he realized that murder was something you never got tired of, which probably accounted for the fact that he had given three decades of his life to it. *News of the World, Daily Express, The Sun* – he'd turned out copy on deadline for all the Fleet Street rags, and he was still at it at *The Sentinel*. The names changed, but the crimes somehow all remained the same. Only now he'd crossed over into not simply reporting on a crime, but investigating it as well. What would be the consequences? Freddie figured he would soon find out.

The sun was sinking fast by the time the bus pulled up along a desolate stretch of Ocean Beach. But it was an overcast day and instead of a smartphone-ready sunset the light was fading to gray, as if someone had thrown a shroud over the sky.

Ritter grabbed the mic, then stood and faced the tourists. "Last stop, folks. This might look like the beach to you, but back in the Seventies it was a killing ground. A serial killer known as The Doodler used to pick men up here, have sex with them, then stab them to death. But as you may have read in the flyer, he liked to sketch their portraits first," Ritter grinned. "I guess we all got our kinks, right?"

The tourists tittered as they exchanged glances.

"Feel free to step off the bus, walk along the beach, take some pics, and try to imagine what it must have been like here when the Doodler was on the hunt."

Ritter sat back down and opened the door. His passengers stood and started shuffling down the aisle toward the door.

"Let's get off," Vivian. "I could use some air."

"Righto," Freddie said.

The tourists filed off the bus and spread out along the beach. By the time Vivian and Freddie reached the door, they were the only passengers on the bus.

"Going somewhere?" Ritter said as they approached the door.

"Yeah, we're getting off. You mind?" Vivian said.

Ritter shook his head. "Yeah, I do mind. You're not going anywhere."

It was then that Vivian remembered where she'd heard his voice before.

"It was you…" she said. "You called me…"

Ritter offered a thin smile. "I tried to warn you, but you wouldn't listen." He closed the door, then pulled a 9mm Glock semiautomatic and pointed it at Vivian and Freddie. "Now it's too late."

SIXTY-NINE

Vivian and Freddie froze at the sight of the gun.

"Sit down," Ritter said.

Freddie and Vivian exchanged glances, then sat down.

"What the devil do you think you're doing?" Freddie said.

"Shut up," Ritter said.

Vivian nodded at the tourists on the beach. "If I scream everybody's gonna hear me."

Ritter leaned in and pressed the muzzle of the gun against Vivian's cheek. "Go ahead. Scream," he said.

"You're a bloody coward if you shoot her!" Freddie blurted out.

Ritter gave a grim smile, then swung the gun at Freddie. "Maybe I should shoot you instead."

"No! Please! Don't!" Vivian said. "We'll do whatever you want, okay?"

"Good," Ritter said. He turned away from Vivian and Freddie and peered under the driver's seat. Freddie took advantage of the opportunity and slipped his hand into his pocket. He reached for his phone, quickly entered his passcode, tapped "Camera," tapped "Video," then slid the phone back into his pocket.

Ritter pulled out a length of coiled clothesline from under the seat. As he did so, Vivian saw her blue lululemon bag.

"Hey, wait a minute – that's my bag…"

Ritter gave her a cold smile. "Don't worry. You won't be needing it where you're going."

"It was you, wasn't it? You tried to run me off the road!"

Ritter ignored Vivian and handed Freddie the clothesline. "Tie her up."

Freddie hesitated. He glanced at Vivian. "Tie her up?"

"Now!" Ritter barked.

"Yes, of course," Freddie said. He uncoiled a length of clothesline and began tying Vivian to her seat. She was trembling, and winced as he tightened the knots. "Sorry, love."

"Shut up!" Ritter barked.

Ritter waited until Floyd had restrained Vivian, then said, "Give me the rope."

Freddie handed it back to him. Ritter used a knife to cut the rope, then pointed to a seat across the aisle.

"You, over there."

Freddie sat down. Ritter glanced out the windshield at the tourists on the beach, then used the rope to tie Freddie to the seat. He worked quickly and when he was finished he stuffed the remaining length of clothesline back under the driver's seat. Then he swung into the seat and turned the key. The bus's diesel engine rattled into life. Ritter shifted into Drive and pulled away. As she glanced out the window, Vivian could see the tourists on the beach waving their arms in the gathering dark and running after the bus with confused and puzzled expressions on their faces.

"Where we going?" Vivian said.

"Last stop on the tour," Ritter said.

Vivian and Freddie exchanged glances.

"This was the last stop," Freddie said.

"I added an extra stop just for you," Ritter said.

SEVENTY

THE HEADLIGHTS SWEPT ACROSS THE BUSES. THERE WERE DOZENS OF them, and they were parked next to each other in a deserted dirt lot that appeared to be a bus graveyard. Vivian and Freddie exchanged glances as Ritter rolled past row after row of rusting, graffiti-splashed school and city buses. She noticed that some of the marquees read SORRY, OUT OF SERVICE, as if anyone had any doubt.

"Where are we?" Vivian said, looking out at the ghostly hulks as the fear climbed into her throat.

Ritter ignored her. He turned down a row of buses and parked next to a derelict school bus. He killed the engine, flipped on the interior lights, then turned and looked at Vivian and Freddie.

"Welcome to the last stop," he said.

"It was you, wasn't it?" Vivian said. "You killed Joanna."

Ritter nodded. "I guess there's no harm in telling you, seeing as you're not gonna get a chance to tell anybody about it."

"Why Joanna?"

"She stole my book."

Vivian and Freddie exchanged glances.

"*Death Trip*? I thought she stole Ben Torrey's book, *Tourist Trap*."

Ritter gave a cold smile. "They both stole it," he said.

I don't understand…"

"I'll make it simple for you," Ritter said. "Ben stole my book and turned it into *Tourist Trap*. Then that bitch Joanna stole *Tourist Trap* and called it *The Murder Tour*."

"Ben didn't kill himself, did he?" Freddie said.

"Let's just say he had some help," Ritter said.

He pulled out his smartphone and held it out so Vivian and Freddie could see a video playing on the screen. A man in his 40s was sitting behind the wheel of a vintage BMW and staring at the camera with a terrified expression on his face. Vivian could see that he was tied up. She could also hear the sound of the engine running.

"What's your name?" a man said.

Vivian recognized the voice as Ritter's.

"Ben Torrey."

"Do you have a confession to make, Ben?"

Torrey nodded.

"Go ahead."

"We stole your book," Torrey said, "me and Sylvia. She found the flash drive with the manuscript on it and gave it to me."

"You pimped her out so you could steal the book, didn't you?"

Torrey nodded.

"Your own wife."

Torrey looked away from the camera, as if to hide his shame.

"Why'd you steal it?"

"We thought we could get away with it."

"You mean you thought you could sell it, right?"

Torrey nodded again.

"But you were wrong," Ritter said.

"Please don't do this…"

"I have to set an example."

Vivian watched in horror as Ritter fed a garden hose into the car, then rolled up the window. Torrey started screaming, but Ritter had apparently turned the sound off. It didn't matter though. Torrey's agonized expression and silent screams made it even more horrifying. The smartphone camera stayed on Torrey until he was overcome by

251

the fumes and slumped in his seat. Vivian leaned forward and vomited on the floor next to her seat.

"You wanted to know," Ritter said. "Now you know."

"What about his wife?" Freddie said. "Did you kill her too?"

"Had to, just to be fair," Ritter said.

"Three people dead, all because of a book?" Vivian said. "Seriously?"

"Not *a* book. *My* book," he said, poking a thumb at himself.

"I read a lot of mysteries and I thought it sucked," Vivian said. "Joanna's version was way better."

Ritter sneered. "I guess you're some kind of expert on mysteries, huh?"

"I know what's good," Vivian said in a defiant tone of voice.

"Yeah, and look what it got you," Ritter said. "You found out the hard way that books and real life got nothing to do with each other."

"Why'd you write it anyway? I thought you were a bus driver."

Ritter shrugged. "Got the idea driving the bus. Guess it was a pretty good one since everybody wanted to steal it." He opened the door and stepped off the bus.

Vivian looked at Freddie, vomit in the corners of her mouth. "I look like shit, don't I, Freddie?"

Freddie tried to smile. He could see the tears in her eyes and knew he could do nothing to console her or ease her fears.

"What's he gonna do?" Vivian said. "Is he gonna kill us too?"

"Take it easy, love," Freddie said. "We're not dead yet."

"I'm sorry I got you mixed up this," she said.

Freddie gave a rueful smile. "I got myself mixed up in it, love."

Vivian could hear Ritter opening and closing the bus's baggage compartment.

"What's he doing?" she said as her fear nearly suffocated her.

Moments later Ritter fed a hose through the open driver's window. Vivian saw it and screamed.

Ritter boarded the bus and looked at her. "Save your breath. Nobody can hear you out here."

"You're gonna kill us, aren't you? Same way you killed Ben Torrey."

"You catch on fast," Ritter said with a mocking smile. He swung into the driver's seat and started the engine.

"You'll never get away with it," Freddie said.

"How do you know?" Ritter said. "You're not gonna be around to find out." He closed the driver's window until it was snug against the hose, then stepped off the bus and closed the door.

SEVENTY-ONE

FREDDIE GLANCED AT VIVIAN. SHE WAS STARING AT THE HOSE PUMPING invisible death into the bus. Her face had taken on a desperate expression and her eyes were white with terror. She was twisting in her seat and frantically struggling to free herself.

"Stop struggling," Freddie said.

Vivian looked at him, tears streaming down her face. "What am I supposed to do, just sit here and die?"

"Sit still and take shallow breaths," Freddie said.

"What's that gonna do?"

"It'll give you more time, love."

"Oh yeah? To do what?"

"Just hang on, I've got an idea."

"I'm feeling dizzy," Vivian said.

Freddie knew that dizziness was one of the symptoms of CO poisoning, along with headaches, weakness, nausea, vomiting and finally unconsciousness. He was starting to feel dizzy himself, and knew that time was running out. He had to act fast if they had any chance of survival. He glanced at Vivian and saw that she was nodding out.

"My head hurts," Vivian said. "Get us out of here, please."

Freddie shifted in his seat as he struggled to reach into his pants pocket. He winced as the clothesline chafed his hand. He glanced at the hose, then forced his hand into his pocket and managed to grab hold of his cigarette lighter. But whether he could pull it out of his pocket was another story. His hand was sweaty and the lighter kept slipping out of his fingers as he tried to pull it out. Finally he managed to hold onto it and carefully pulled it out of his pocket. Now the challenge was to flick it without dropping it.

"Freddie…" Vivian said. She was woozy and slipping into unconsciousness.

"Hang on, love," Freddie said. "Almost there."

Freddie managed to flick the lighter, wincing as the flame singed his hand. Then he held it against the clothesline until it started to burn. After what seemed like an eternity, the clothesline came apart and he was able to free his hand. He worked quickly to untie himself, glancing out the door to see if Ritter was coming. But all he saw was darkness.

He finished untying himself and moved to untie Vivian. His dizziness was getting worse and he had a splitting headache, but he knew he had to keep going.. Then he heard Ritter approaching the bus. He arranged the clothesline loosely around Vivian to make it appear as if she was still restrained, then went back to his seat and slumped against the window with the clothesline draped around him.

He saw Ritter board the bus, only now he was wearing a respirator and carrying what appeared to be a can of gasoline in one hand and a cigarette lighter in the other. With his eyes half-closed, Freddie watched as Ritter began moving down the aisle, swinging the can from side to side and splashing gasoline on the seats. Freddie waited until Ritter was almost upon him, then sprang to his feet and rushed him. Ritter grunted, taken by surprise. He fell backwards, and as he did so the can tipped and he drenched himself with gasoline. Struggling to regain his footing, Ritter accidentally flicked the lighter. He screamed as he erupted in flames.

Freddie grabbed Vivian and dragged her toward the door as fire engulfed the bus. Flames were licking at her clothes as they stumbled off the bus. They collapsed on the ground and Freddie rolled on top of Vivian to snuff out the flames.

"What happened...?" Vivian said. She was half-conscious and slurring her words.

"We're alive, love, that's what happened," Freddie said, glancing at the bus. He could feel the heat from the fire raging out of control. "But we have to get out of here before the whole place goes up."

"Outta where?" Vivian slurred.

Freddie managed to pull her to her feet and, with her arm around his neck and his arm around her waist, he dragged her away from the buses and toward the barbed wire fence that surrounded the graveyard. By the time they got there the fire had spread to the other buses in the yard, and when Freddie turned and looked back at the blaze, the entire graveyard was a raging inferno lighting up the night sky.

They sank to the ground by the fence. Freddie waited until he could catch his breath, then pulled out his cell phone and managed to tap 911 before he passed out.

SEVENTY-TWO

Vivian and Freddie sat in the back of the ambulance wrapped in blankets. The paramedics had treated them for burns and now they were wearing oxygen masks and breathing pure oxygen, which over time would replace the carbon monoxide in their blood. Freddie had managed to get them out of the bus before they developed more serious cases of CO poisoning, and now they just had to wait until their bodies returned to normal. They had been wearing the masks for three hours and, according to the paramedics, they would be in the clear after four hours of pure oxygen.

Detectives Bassett and Chen were there as well, impatiently waiting for the opportunity to interview Vivian and Freddie. As she waited, Vivian looked around the bus yard. It looked as if it had been firebombed. Firefighters and emergency personnel were moving through the black smoke and charred hulks of burned-out buses, mopping up after an inferno that had turned the bus yard into a wasteland and Floyd Ritter into ashes.

Vivian glanced at Freddie, who affectionately squeezed her hand. He had saved her life, and she would never forget it. Nor would she ever forget Floyd Ritter. She smiled to herself as she realized that they had survived because Freddie hadn't quit smoking and still had his cigarette lighter. Not only that, he also had the presence of mind to know how to use it. She had repeatedly urged him to quit, but owed her life to the fact that he never took her advice.

An hour later the masks came off and Bassett and Chen moved in to question Vivian and Freddie.

"How you feeling?" Chen said

"Better," Vivian said.

"You couldn't stay away from it, could you?" Bassett said.

Vivian threw Bassett a defiant look. "We got him, didn't we? We got the guy who killed Joanna and Ben and Sylvia Torrey."

"Is that right?"

"Yeah, that's right."

"It's just your word against his, and he ain't talking," Bassett said, a skeptical look on her face.

"I expect you'll want to know what happened," Freddie said. "Perhaps this will help." He pulled his cell phone out of his pocket and played the video he had recorded while they were on the bus.

Bassett and Chen stared at the screen and watched as Ritter confessed to killing Joanna and the Torreys, then looked up at Freddie.

"How in the hell did you manage that?" Chen said.

Freddie shrugged. "Just a lucky break, I reckon."

"How'd you know he was the one?" Bassett said.

"We didn't – until he tried to kill us."

Bassett shook her head. "Three people dead because of a book."

Vivian nodded. "Yeah, weird, huh?"

"I'll tell you what's even weirder," Bassett said, frowning.

"What's that?"

"That a couple of amateurs broke the case."

Vivian and Freddie exchanged smiles.

"We'll need you to come down to the station and provide a full report," Chen said.

"Sure, no problem," Vivian said.

"We ought to charge you with interfering with police business," Bassett said.

Vivian looked up at her. "C'mon, Detective, give us a break. We got the guy, didn't we?"

"You should've come to us first."

"We didn't know for sure until we were on the bus," Freddie said, "and by then it was too late."

Bassett and Chen exchanged glances, then Bassett said, "Next time we will charge you."

"Not to worry, Detective, there won't be a next time," Freddie said.

Bassett scoffed. "I'm not so sure with you two."

SEVENTY-THREE

FREDDIE STARED MOROSELY INTO HIS PINT OF GUINNESS.

Vivian took a swig from her mug and looked at him. "What's the matter?"

They were sitting at the bar at The Pig and Whistle, sharing pints in the middle of the afternoon. They had filed their reports with the SFPD earlier in the day, and now there was nothing left to do but celebrate.

"Well, it's over now, isn't it, love?" Freddie said.

"Yeah, we did it."

"Yes, but what I mean is, there's nothing left for us now, is there?"

"You and me?"

"Yes, we were on the case, and now it's done. I filed my story and that's the end of it."

"Maybe not."

Freddie looked at her. "Say what?"

"I mean maybe there'll be another case."

Freddie smiled. "Lovely of you to think so, but we're not detectives, even if we did crack the case. Anyway, don't you have to get a job?"

Vivian nodded sadly. "Yeah, I do. Can't expect my sister to keep paying my rent. Next thing I know she'll want me to move in with her and the kids."

"So it's back to advertising?"

Vivian shrugged. "It's the only thing I know how to do."

"Hold on now, I reckon you're rather a good gumshoe too."

Vivian grinned. "Yeah, we're a good team, you and me, Freddie."

"So maybe we should keep working together," Freddie said.

Vivian took on a puzzled expression. "How?"

"You and me, working together at *The Sentinel*."

Vivian's eyes lit up. "You mean as a crime reporter?"

Freddie nodded. "What do you say, love? I think I can swing it now that I broke the story for the paper."

"That would be fantastic!" Vivian said. She threw her arms around Freddie. "When do I start?"

"Soon as I clear it with Tom."

"Woo hoo!" Vivian said and raised her mug. "I'll drink to that!"

"As shall I," Freddie said. They clinked mugs and sipped their ale.

Vivian wiped her mouth and looked over at two patrons who were playing darts.

"I want you to teach me how to play darts."

Freddie looked at her. "Darts?"

"Yeah, it looks like fun."

Freddie nodded at her Guinness. "Darts. Guinness. You're liable to turn into a right proper Brit."

Vivian grinned. "Hey, we're partners, aren't we?"

They were walking back to Freddie's Jag when Vivian's cell phone rang. She pulled it out of her pocket and glanced at the screen.

"Are you kidding me?" she said.

Freddie looked at her. "What is it?"

Vivian put the phone on speaker, then took the call.

"Hey Donny, what's up?" she said.

"Hey Vivian, how's it going?"

"How's it going? Seriously? You fired me, remember? That's how it's going."

"Yeah, look, that's what I wanted to talk to you about." Donny paused, then said, "I want you to come back."

"You mean the client wants me to come back, right?"

"I'll be honest with you, Viv. They're gonna walk if you're not on the business."

"Sorry, Donny, I'm making a career change."

"What are you talking about, career change? You're a copywriter."

"Not anymore," Vivian said. She glanced at Freddie. "I'm a crime reporter at *The San Francisco Sentinel*."

"What?"

"Good luck with the business, Donny. You're gonna need it."

Vivian ended the call and slipped the phone into her pocket. Freddie opened the Jag's door on the passenger side.

"After you, milady," he said with a bow.

Vivian grinned and got in the car. Freddie went around to the driver's side and climbed in behind the wheel. He turned the key, then smiled as the engine miraculously sprang into life. Moments later, with Freddie at the wheel, *The San Francisco Sentinel*'s newest crime reporter drove off to her next assignment.

Dear reader,

We hope you enjoyed reading *Murder Goes on Tour*. Please take a moment to leave a review, even if it's a short one. Your opinion is important to us.

Discover more books by Robert Baty at
https://www.nextchapter.pub/authors/robert-baty

Want to know when one of our books is free or discounted? Join the newsletter at
http://eepurl.com/bqqB3H

Best regards,

Robert Baty and the Next Chapter Team

ABOUT THE AUTHOR

Robert Baty is the author of a mystery series set in the world of classic cars. "Fast, Beautiful and Dangerous," the first book in the series, was published by TouchPoint Press in 2019. The second book in the series, "The Beauty in the Bay," will be released in 2021. Bob lives in the Oakland Hills above San Francisco, and when he's not following his characters down the mean streets of his imagination, he's piloting his vintage Alfa Romeo through the blind curves that lie just ahead.

Lightning Source UK Ltd.
Milton Keynes UK
UKHW041832120321
380264UK00007B/385/J